Married
to the
Mahr

AUTHOR'S NOTE

This novel contains content that may be sensitive. Due to the rules and restrictions of publishing with the 'zon, lease always read the description of content on the author's website.

This is a work of fiction. Names, characters, places, and incidents either are the product of the author's imagination or are used fictitiously. Any resemblance to actual persons, living or dead, events, or locales is entirely coincidental.

Copyright © 2023 Delilah Dare

All rights reserved. No part of this book may be reproduced or used in any manner without written permission of the copyright owner except for the use of quotations in a book review.

First edition published 2023

Cover illustrations copyright © 2023 by Rosel Graphic Designs
Edited by Lawrence Editing

Published by Delilah Dare
www.delilahdarebooks.com

To everyone whose nightmares could use a lot more kissing.

When striking a deal with a demon, you do not write the rules.

Chapter 1
Addison

The gaudy blue house with its peeling paint and crooked shutters taunted Addison from the driveway. This was the third day she'd come home from work at the Something Fishy Market & Diner to the rental that was big enough for a family.

The slam of her car door trapped her puffy mauve coat and the accompanying sound of fabric ripping from seam to armpit brought a surge of fresh rage to her cheeks. Her coworkers already teased her for wearing a heavy coat in Boston's spring season while everyone else wore jackets and raincoats.

The front door required a hefty jiggle and a full-body slam just to do its job. The inside of the house was an improvement from the outside, but it was all nauseating to Addison. The lonely house was one big, glaring reminder of her failed relationship, which she's sure was her fault, and not just because Justin literally told her it was.

It's true that hindsight is a different pair of glasses. Her view while they were together was rosy and pink, whereas now she looked back to see the rosy red clay coating the lenses was actually a big smear of dung and it was honestly shocking she hadn't walked right off a cliff to her death. She'd held onto the relationship even after it became one-sided, had comforted herself with his physical nearness while he'd been light years away and growing farther with each breath. It was the idea of being needed that she admired the most about Justin; more than the man himself, she longed to be useful as much as she dreaded being alone. His many attempts at confrontation had been easily parried with her extensive training in avoidance of conflict, so well deflected that she didn't even realize what was happening until he texted her *I can't do this* the day they were meant to move from his one-bedroom apartment to a roomy house.

Memories of her beachside flat and her best friend, Marissa, back in Florida flooded her broken heart as she surveyed the boxes and tubs that littered the floor. Justin's poor credit obligated Addison to sign the lease, essentially trapping her here for a full year. Anyone who's gone from renting an apartment to a house knows the transformation comes with a whole lot *more*—more cleaning, more pride, more bills, more money, more overwhelming depression when the walls could house an entire loving family, and yet there was no one else there, just Addison, utterly alone. Strategically placed Bluetooth speakers that constantly blared music helped fill the empty space and drown her thoughts, but only as much as they'd helped as a kid with her mom's shenanigans in the next room.

It was a long day at the fish market and Addison was exhausted, but sleep hadn't been kind lately. It hadn't been friendly for most of her life. Her earliest memory of a nightmare went hand in hand with her earliest memory, which featured the rise and fall of her mother's voice in a boisterous, drunken fight with a boyfriend Addison didn't recall. The sound of raised voices and shattering glass lodged their way into her dream and shaped the nightmares that followed her from bed to bed, fluidly restructuring to add the horrors that came along with living as she grew up. The night terrors worsened when she was stressed out, depressed, or ate too much chocolate.

With a sigh, she tossed her work clothes directly into the washer—admittedly a perk of having the whole house to herself—and headed to the shower. The stench of fish and whatever chemicals her boss used to package and freeze the largemouth bass, black crappie, redbreast sunfish, and many other varieties of slimy, icky, smelly ocean creatures that she wished she didn't know so much about clung to her clothes every day. If she skipped a shower even once, she was sure the smelly particles would burrow its way into her pillow and then rub itself deep into her pores and follicles as she slept, and in the morning she would wake up and see a half-fish humanoid staring at her from the mirror.

After a moderately timed shower—long enough to clean off but quick enough not to be concerning come time to pay bills—Addison plopped down at her fully assembled worktable. Her sanctuary. Neatly spread upon the desk were tarot cards for easy morning readings, a framed photo of the view from her old apartment, her laptop, and a wish jar for manifesting her deepest desires. Oh, and Steve.

"Hey, Stevie." The anatomical figurine waved back as she flicked his wooden hand to and fro.

Her latest work in progress was already on the screen the moment she opened her laptop, a book cover for her friend's cozy witch mystery series. This was the second cover in a trilogy for Marissa, whose beautiful covers had the advantage of her entire graphic design degree channeled into one sole project. Thank goodness Addison spent many years and dollars learning to make a handful of covers and a smattering of character art for one client.

Sarcasm aside, the bills in her name obstructed any dreams she may have had for starting up a business venture or building a clientele in a competitive field like graphic design. The move to Boston was solely to be with Justin, and the fish market was the only decent-paying job that she was adequately underqualified for, and it would take all her time busting ass and slinging fish to keep up this stupid family house.

Maybe I'll get a roommate. The obscene and yet upsettingly logical thought intruded her wandering mind and plunked a fresh stone of anxiety to the spot between her ribs.

Addison didn't notice she'd fallen asleep until the scene unfolding around her became eerily familiar. Halloween circa thirteen years ago, twelve-year-old Addy and her longtime frenemies planned and coordinated their outfits with the theme of Beauty and the Beast after watching the animated film at a sleepover weeks beforehand. Her two closest friends and biggest bullies dressed up as Belle while she'd gone as the beast. The bratty girls had spent all night mercilessly teasing her for picking the wrong character.

"You knew we were going as Belle! You just want to kiss us, don't you?"

The worst part was, she did have a little crush on one of them. The kind a pubescent girl gets on her friends that could grow into more if nurtured or be stamped out with anti-rhetoric, prejudice, and bullying, until that part of her was so buried she wasn't sure what to name it.

God, they were so annoying. The part of Addison aware that she was in a nightmare watched, thinking of how she wished she'd dropped them and never spoken to them again after that night. Unfortunately, the awful friendship lasted well through junior year of high school.

Truthfully, she'd gone as the beast because she was utterly taken by him. Every time she watched the movie, she longed to be in Belle's place, studying the way he reacted to his human love. She often rewound the movie before the ending where he turned back into the prince, preferring to pretend that part never happened.

At a young age, she started showing signs of an active sexuality, which she'd spent a long time feeling ashamed of. But who cares? She admitted it now, proudly: *I'd totally bang that manbeast*.

But in the nightmare, her mind and body weren't so progressive yet and her whole being was permeated with shame and guilt. She was that preteen again, hiding her feelings and wishing to be *anywhere else*, to be relieved from the endless humiliation that is puberty.

Vague awareness dawned on her. The dream had gone on long enough that something really wicked was bound to happen soon. Sure enough, the edges of her foggy vision began to blur. Menacing darkness pooled in the corners of the dreamscape, accumulating in magnitude until a great tsunami wave rose behind her childhood friends. She turned on her heel and tried to run, but every step she took met the ground like a treadmill. A fluffy gray kitten appeared at her feet, rubbing and mewling innocently. Addison snatched the baby into her arms and pushed her legs, but she could not move. Panic froze the breath inside her lungs. She recalled her high school track meets and attempted to scale the insurmountable distance like a hurdle, but that only landed her flat on her face.

Fear blared inside her mind like a surround-sound alarm. She clawed against the sand, but her hands only sank. She could hear the kitten crying somewhere but could not reach it.

Resigned to her fate, she rolled onto her back and faced the wave. It was different now; she could make out warped faces stretched and exaggerated within the writhing crest. The intermingled demons collided and morphed, their bodies made up of both a nebulous black and a sickly boil-covered plague. She braced herself for the wave of pestilence to smother her, to suffocate her and peel off her skin, to leak into every orifice of her body.

Nothing happened.

The dream dissipated unexpectedly. She felt a thump against her chest and was sent sailing down a flight of winding stairs, her knees occasionally bumping into hard stone on the way down. Her surroundings were dark, but nothing lurked in that darkness. It was simply void of light, not a writhing conglomeration of disease and shame. As her dreamland body took the relentless beating, she thought, *this is marginally better*.

At the bottom of the staircase, she woke with a groan and peeled her face off the keyboard. Still addled with exhaustion, she decided to go to bed and hoped for more of…whatever that nightmare had been. She shed her sweatpants, climbed onto the full-sized mattress she'd purchased with money that should've gone to the gas bill, and settled into the oversized comforter.

As she closed her eyes, the last thing she noticed was a little butterfly trapped in her room. Through her brain fog, she felt it was a kindred spirit. She drifted into captivity in the land of dreams, content to pretend the pretty insect would keep her safe.

Chapter 2
Traeyr

Shadows clung to Traeyr as he hunted the densely populated human settlement. He passed a house with lights still on inside. The human dwelling there cast a shadow that attempted to flee its owner in favor of his dark presence, but he moved on too quickly for it to take hold.

Traeyr has hunted the globe from axis to axis for centuries, marveling at the way things changed. Species died, overtaken by the rise of a new kind, and technologies eliminated the memory of the old; while the earth persevered and fabricated new ways to thrive in the wake of the latest tyrannical genus.

In all his marvelous travels, never had there been a population so ripe for his influence as this land. The humans were packed into high-rising towers of glass that housed farms of sleepers prime for midday meals, a luxury he'd never experienced so frequently until the turn of recent centuries. Farmers and field workers of the past didn't sleep during the day, while now there was an abundance of anxious humans dressed in uptight clothes poring over wasteful resources at any time of day just waiting to be harvested. Their nightmares were easily concocted and nutritiously filling and kept him coming back every few decades despite its unappealing landscape.

People dreamed of witless things. Traeyr used to be a curious pup and lapped up the ambitious dreams, the silly, wacky, ridiculous things, using them to divine what was happening in the real world. One trip around the globe proved how insignificant each dream and its dreamer truly were. The revelation turned his curiosity to the beauty of nature instead, a much more rewarding pastime and a largely more deserving object of his interest.

Traeyr's existence was a wonder, a phenomenon that should have never been possible to create and a painful reminder of what he lost. Humans, on the other hand, were simply farms. Each and every one held its own yield of crops, some tastier than others and some that didn't cultivate any dreams on their own and required a green thumb to coax the terror lurking inside to the surface for Traeyr's consumption.

An unsuspecting sleeper whimpered under his weight. Hungry but bored, Traeyr leaned his elbows on his knees and plucked the bitter taste of the sleeper's nightmare absently. Shadows from under the bed reached for him and he flicked them away with irritation, eager to feed and retreat far from the human inhabitance.

A tantalizing smell wafted to his senses from a crack in the window seal. He dragged in a long breath that made his spine straighten and caused him to lose connection with the sleeper under his legs. A bizarre emotion rippled through him, an excitement he couldn't remember the name of.

His power condensed on his command and he rushed through the tight space of the keyhole, the pleasure of fitting through the small opening heightening his exhilaration. He must taste the savory treat that could perfume the air from so far away, determined to claim the delicious nightmare for his own and mark the home of the sleeper capable of such a delicacy.

Perhaps he would see what they would produce if he truly lost himself, crushing them to release every last drop of their delectable notes. Snapping the bones of a sleeper with his weight while they were possessed by a naturally formed and fully developed nightmare released an undiluted essence that surpassed what he could get by manipulating dreams himself or by leaving sleepers unscathed. By the smell of this one, he would be well sated if he left only a corpse behind.

His hunt for the sleeper took peculiarly long and he found himself doubting himself. How could he have possibly smelled a dream from so far away? Yet, the strength of its tempting fragrance did not fade. It grew nearer and nearer until he finally reached a little blue house in a neighborhood miles away.

The keyhole was unclogged, which was the norm. Humans had long ago forgotten the existence of his kind. It used to be that mahrs and others of dark persuasion would search for an opening, sometimes traveling over oceans and deserts just to get inside for a meal. For Traeyr, going without a decent meal for so long meant spending less time semi-corporeal and more as a depleted, slow-moving butterfly of shade.

Traeyr felt every hard bump and ridge of the aperture as he slunk through the compact space, the most comparable sensation to mortal pleasure he was capable of experiencing.

Hair the color of a maple leaf at the end of autumn cascaded in rivulets over her neck and desk. Her voluptuous body was curled over itself where she cradled her head in the crook of her arm, and Traeyr was struck by the thought that she was a picture of beauty. A nonsensical thought, as he had no idea what the human standard of beauty was these days. Nor ever for that fact, having never subscribed to them himself. The combination of her sleeping form and her ability to conjure such an enticing dream made her worthy of the word beautiful in his mind.

The dreamer clenched her fist against the table and tilted her face toward him. Her lip quivered and her forehead creased, all signs of a powerful and substantial nightmare that could sustain him enough for his trip to the mountains. He found himself rooted in place with an ache where his soul would be if he still owned one.

A glimmer of sweat dotted the line where her hair met her scalp. The moisture caught Traeyr's eye and awakened something primal in his core.

Just a taste.

One luxurious lick of her widow's peak sent shivers through him, a thrill that raced through the wisps of his shadow form. The potency of her liquid exploded his condensed power from within, sending a surge of energy from the tips of his horns to the points of his claws until he was nearly at full mass.

As quickly as his full form materialized, it shrank back down like the snap of a rubber band until he regained control and settled somewhere in between. He stared in astonishment at the creature whose dreams smelled like a bushel of wild berries and whose fluid alone could do what typically required weeks of feeding. What was she?

What else could she do?

The sleeper moaned restlessly in the throes of her nightmare, which released another wave of flourishing scents through his senses. He poised to slurp down the dream and then paused. If he ate the fully formed, naturally occurring nightmare, he stood to gain a brawny chunk of power. However, it would inevitably make the nightmare plunge deeper into the depths of horror tailor-made for its dreamer.

He could relieve the human from the nightmare that plagued her. He could even transform it into a dream of good fortune, a fantasy filled with all of her mortal desires.

Last time he'd given in to his pity, a greedy farmer who blamed him for torturing his wife trapped him—although Traeyr suspected the man had been jealous that he was riding her chest in the night. Unfortunately, the farmer had been a close acquantance of the man who had cursed Traeyr into a nightmare-eating demon and easily hunted down Traeyr's name and his mother's address. Armed with this knowledge and full of greed, he trapped Traeyr and compelled him to perform the ritual that bound him to their bedroom. He had spent many years in that room, forced to construct dreams that were better than their humdrum reality. It was agonizing and irritating beyond belief for Traeyr, who was meant to wander with the breeze.

The human sniffled. Her forehead wrinkled so deeply it looked abrasive. Unable to watch her worry over such a menial thing as a nightmare a moment longer, he reached for the dream and eased it away from the personalized hellscape. He would not risk being held captive again, but he could ease her suffering in this minuscule fashion.

The modification of her dream meant imbibing a sliver of its power. The slight nibble of her nightmare coursed through him much like her sweat, but this time he braced for it and was able to enjoy the honeyed taste of her saccharine nectar. He licked his lips as it passed through his awareness and mourned the sacrifice of a full feast of such palatable taste.

This will not be my only taste, he vowed in an effort to appease his growing hunger.

Stirred from sleep by the sudden change in her dream, the sleeper woke under his touch. Traeyr minimized himself into the trusty butterfly and stuck to the shadows as she shed a layer of clothing and sleepily stumbled to the bed. She lay with one leg out of the blanket crooked at the knee, face-down on the pillow, a position that would not allow Traeyr to ride her properly. He would have to convince her to roll onto her back, which he considered attempting for a moment but decided against. He wouldn't risk crushing her right after doing her such kindness as foregoing a delicious evening meal in place of her simple comfort.

He watched ruefully as she twitched in her sleep. The soft pants of her breath steeled his determination. He wanted more than her sweat and hair, he wanted to taste what wonders lay in her mind. He imagined the flavorful mix of spices and textures of emotions he would savor from each bite of her.

With the envisaged dessert sending need through every fiber of his being, his thoughts wandered to her flesh. The soft pink hues of her cheeks and the raised bumps on her arms. He skittered his shadow across her exposed leg and watched the reaction of her flesh to his touch with ravenous enthusiasm.

Oh, yes, he would devour her.

Nightmares and all.

Chapter 3
Addison

Addison roused moments before her alarm started its vibrating blare from all the way across the room on the desk. She remained in bed for a few moments to allow her brain to develop a sense of its surroundings and sever her from any lingering night terrors.

Slowly, it dawned on her that her mind wasn't as addled with terrors as it usually was upon waking. While her dreams had been full of nightmares as always, the scope of them was nowhere near the usual atrocities she endured while unconscious. They all felt like cookie-cutter bad dreams that belonged to normal people, people who'd gone through life without experiencing a single traumatic event. Falling down stairs, showing up to work naked, failing a test. That sort of thing. The dreams were a huge relief compared to her typically gory—and frankly downright abusive—dreams, a hodgepodge of current stressors, bone-deep insecurities, and past traumas, with a heaping helping of death, fear, and carnage strewn throughout. Her typical night was about survival, not embarrassment.

In fact, she woke with a slickness between her legs. She hadn't been horny for months, even before Justin dumped her. Ever since he'd called her a needy lover, her river had run dry. Apparently, that kind of thing gnaws away at a person's libido.

Addison was not about to let the moment slip away. She threw off the comforter, rose from the bed like a giddy teenager, tossed her soaked panties in the washer, and dug through the boxes and tubs strewn about the bedroom in search of her trusty vibrator. Once the pink apparatus of orgasms was in her hand, she arranged the pillows just so and sat on the bed propped against the wall.

She used the tips of her nails to trace the curve of her stomach, allowing her light touch to tease her deeper need and build her arousal. With her eyes closed, she pretended the soft caress was that of a willing lover, someone who found the extra curves on her body appealing and not repulsive as her last lover had.

Justin flickered in her mind and she shot her eyes open, determined not to let him ruin this. She rocked her hips to remind her body of the goal. With one hand caressing her breast and pinching her nipples, she ran the other down to her opening and slid a finger through her slick folds. She slid the toy against her liquid heat, rubbing against it to coat it before teasing herself with its entry.

A faint shadow near the doorknob stole her attention. Her heart skipped a beat, certain someone was about to walk in until she remembered she lived alone. Instead of allowing the hiccup to steal away her hunger, she let it build her desire.

Would you like a show? She raised her knees and rocked against her toy, keeping steady pressure on her pert nipple as she delved it into her slick folds, guiding her slickness up to the nub of her clit. Her hips bucked and her heart quickened and she didn't dampen her moans of pleasure as she chased her release. She rode her vibrator until her hips clenched and her arm locked in place, her climax stealing the breath from her lungs.

The rest of the morning was spent at her desk with Steve, a plate of bacon, and Halsey's comforting croon filling the room while she fiddled with Marissa's cover. The design was coming along, albeit slowly, but her outlook was a little brighter. Maybe this new situation wasn't as bad as she thought.

Maybe it was a blessing that Justin dumped her before moving in together. Even her morning tarot card reading seemed to agree. She certainly wouldn't have had an orgasm this morning if he were living in the same house.

"Hey, Addy! Thanks for working for me yesterday," Leah said. She bumped her hip on Addison's and smiled up at her from her four-and-a-half-foot stature. "You're a great friend. Text me if you need any shifts covered this week. Just give me, like, a couple hours' notice if you can."

"Thanks, but I need the money. Let me know if I can pick up any more of yours, too. I'm happy to help."

Over Leah's shoulder, Nasty Nathan threw open the swinging kitchen doors. Her mood soured as his gaze rose from Leah's ass to her own chest. In a lowered voice, she warned her friend, "Look out."

Leah's empathetic gaze flicked to hers before she scurried away. Addison made to follow, but a greasy hand landed on her shoulder. Her body curled inward as she ducked from his grip, and she noticed with a cringe that he was—once again—not wearing the plastic gloves everyone was supposed to have on at all times. This was a fish market, for goodness' sake. No wonder her clothes always stunk, with her disgusting boss manhandling her whenever he pleased.

"You're late. Again."

What the hell are you talking about, you psycho? Addison was literally *never* late. This dead-end job was all she had. Overqualified or not, she couldn't risk losing the income.

"No, I'm not." She yanked her shoulder free of his sausage fingers.

His stern expression lightened and he chuckled. "All right, all right. Get back to work."

Ugh. So it had all been a ploy just to touch her. Gross. Between his lingering looks at every woman in the vicinity and the way he ogled her breasts, plus his putrid breath and handsiness, Nasty Nathan reminded

Addison of the men who always happened to be at her childhood home. Even being near him made her skin crawl and her arms cross over her chest, just as she'd done when it became obvious that she was maturing faster than other girls back then.

The cloud of contentment that had lingered after her orgasmic morning dissipated. The good mood had made her thirty-minute drive one of loud music and off-key singing and left a blithe smile on her lips for the first few customers of the day.

Now she turned toward the couple at the counter with a sneer that she struggled to shake. Her thoughts turned to Florida, to her old apartment, and to her closest friend. *I just have to make it through this year.*

Obviously Florida wouldn't be any cheaper, but it was home, and she would happily share the rent with Marissa. With creative opportunities abound, she was more likely to find something that utilized her passion. Marissa was the only one who knew firsthand everything she'd dealt with growing up and loved her anyway, even after the cesspit of depression Addison had gone through after finally getting out on her own. Marissa was family, her only family in many senses of the word.

Hell, I'd even move back in with Mom for a few weeks if I had to. This thought didn't ring quite as true, though. Her mom was surely still on the coast somewhere, probably in need of some spare cash for a fresh bottle. Somehow the woman paid her rent and yet always needed to borrow money from Addison.

Work dragged on until the clock surpassed eight o'clock. Twenty minutes later, Olivia rushed in to relieve her. Addison forced a polite smile at her coworker, who she was pretty sure was allowed to be late whenever she pleased due to her shameless flirting with Nasty Nathan, but the extra minutes on Addison's time card were worth it.

When she got home and after she took a shower, she blasted the speakers on shuffle and slunk into her computer chair. After some time of irritated fussing with the book cover, she decided to drop it and do some much-needed unpacking instead.

The noisy music barely pierced the incessant ramblings of her mind, the loop of thoughts that were always present when she was alone more powerful than any Bluetooth speaker. The sound seemed not to penetrate her eardrums as she worked her way through a box of clothes.

Movement at the window cut through her humming and she furrowed her brow at the sight of a little butterfly flitting around the room.

The ends of the wispy black butterfly were undefined and seemed to flicker like the flame of a candle. Tendrils of shadow winked in and out of existence at the tips of the impossible insect, and its wings didn't appear to flap nearly as often as ordinary monarchs. Entranced, Addison reached out and let the beautiful creature land on her finger. It fluttered over her skin and drifted up her arm, leaving a trail of bumps all the way to its perch on her chest.

A strange sense of familiarity tugged at her consciousness, like the foggy memories of a dream right after waking. The details were obscured and it was more a feeling than a formed thought, leaving her to wonder if she was already asleep.

Her body was suddenly too heavy to operate. She waded through molasses to reach the bed, slipped out of her sweatpants, and nestled into the covers.

Chapter 4
Traeyr

Thoughts of the human pervaded his mind all day. He was distracted and inattentive to his hunt, leaving behind a trail of half-cocked nightmares and nearly absentmindedly crushing multiple people to death with his heedlessness.

He conjured her into his mind's eye as she was the morning before. Even her daydreams had mesmerized his senses. The combination of her fantasies and her desire was too great to ignore, heightened by the way she'd crested over the precipice from his mere presence in her bedroom. He knew it had nothing to do with him, but she'd seemed to put on a show especially for his viewing, and that show had burned within him a fire that had him missing his flesh and bones. He wanted to touch her, to aid her in her quest of achieving her highest climax.

When she'd returned to her abode with a gloom hanging over her like a swollen storm cloud, he felt a fierce bolt of protectiveness of her thoughts. If she continued to feel dejected, he knew her dreams would weave themselves around the melancholic emotions and drag her under like a starving kraken faced with a grand ship. Knowing the way these things went, he couldn't help but feel she was being stolen from him. He decided that nothing else, be it demon or her own psyche, was allowed to have that kind of power of this dreamer. Nothing but he could influence her dreams, be it day or night, good or bad. Her stimulating nectar was his to devour, to taste, and his alone.

The female noticed his presence in her bedroom at last. A flicker of something crossed her exquisite features and her brow creased in recognition. Ah, so she had seen him before, but was it possible she could recall him now? The wild notion made his empty heart cavity thrum with anticipation. Humans should not be able to remember their encounters with night demons except in the vague sense of a fading dream. Regardless, he approached her outstretched hand and poured his influence into her subconscious until she hovered in the land between wakefulness and his realm. She removed her unnecessary layer of clothing and lay on her back this time, allowing him to perch carefully on her chest.

He observed her dainty mortal features with greater intent this time. The way her slight nose rounded at the end, a smattering of faint freckles that discolored her cheeks in a most delightful way, her full eyelashes closing over rich eyes that reminded him of the rare bloom of a speckled brown cattleya orchid.

He felt her nightmare take form around the edge of her sleeping mind and watched her eyes oscillate behind her eyelids. He drank the lapping tide of her bad dream and felt a rising wave of gratification, but it fell short. The faint nibble of her scrumptious nightmare was not enough to solidify him and he briefly wondered why he didn't allow himself more, but he knew the answer. He wanted to savor her, to take his time with the dreamer and relish the nourishment she provided. He didn't want to worsen her unconscious experience by taking too much.

Another sliver of her dream delved into him, sending a shockwave of need that pulsed and pushed the boundaries of his control, sending him reeling between shadow and material just like the taste of her hair had.

I must not get carried away. He pulled back and forced the climatic wave down, cinching tight around his power. The pain of restricting himself ached even as it sent thrills through him. He edged closer to the sensation of *fullness*, then backed away, repeating this process while his more corporeal vessel grew in substance and his mind reeled with the continued denial of his release of power. It began to feel like a game, sacrificing a filling meal just to skirt the rim of what he knew would bring him sustenance. He felt as alive as he could only assume he'd once felt before he was transformed into a demon.

He hovered above her as he regained control, vigilant against squashing her under his weight, then perched atop her breasts once more to await the next delectable surge. Liquid pooled in the divot of her eye. It gained speed and traced the seam of her tightly closed lashes until the plump drop came to rest above her cheekbone.

Traeyr watched the tear with ambivalence. He'd been too enraptured by his primal urges to realize her nightmare was seeping past his protection and enveloping her soul. As he morphed her dream into a less intimate nightmare, his primal side remained engrossed with the leakage on her cheek.

I shan't be careless.

With great care, he leaned down to sniff the shimmering liquid. The edges of his semi-corporeal form rippled with glee, his instincts insisting he release control and give in to temptation. Dragging in a settling gulp of air, he slackened his posture in the hope that remaining relaxed would keep him from losing himself. He was old, very old, but centuries of crushing mortals in their sleep and sating himself on their dreams did not prepare him for keeping one of those mortals safe. He was operating on sheer willpower.

With the utmost care, he leaned to the soft curve of her cheek and lapped up the salty fluid.

Oh! *Oh!*

The taste of her sent convulsions through him, his body bursting outward from his core. The shadowy tips of his claws momentarily solidified. His hands fell to either side of the human's head and dug into the cotton fabric above her shoulders. Pleasure gripped every fiber of his being down to his lost soul and wracked with relentless waves of bliss. He fought against the swells of ecstasy, but the battle was futile until the power died down. His body refused his attempts to tamper it and his knees slid to straddle her chest. He rocked forward unintentionally, driving his passion over the dreamer.

The sleeper's eyes snapped wide and her mouth opened in a muted scream. Mortified, Traeyr shoved the overwhelming emotion down and forced his power to obey, condensing until her limbs and her scream were freed. With her shriek echoing behind him, he soared through the house and squeezed through the chinked knob with none of the typical sense of pleasure it elicited. The small crevice was nothing compared to the human's dreams, her essence, her liquid. What had he been thinking? He could have crushed her and all of her spilled fluids and nutritious nightmares would have died with her.

He was not worried she would remember him and go searching for the old legends of his kind. Humans were a forgetful sort, and these centuries they blamed their own minds for afflictions caused by demons and night creatures. No, his fear was internal. An infatuation this strong for a sleeper was inappropriate and damnable. Already he felt empty without the rush of power imbibed with her liquid. If he developed an addiction, it would inevitably lead him to drain the human of her soul, crushing her body, and where would that leave him? Empty and alone, forced to return to feasting on everyday humans with their boring, unsatisfying nightmares, mostly of his own making. Besides, even if he filled up on her power and formed his most solid shadow body, the mass of shadows was a poor imitation of flesh and bone and would never amount to the feeling of flesh-on-flesh that her liquid caused him to crave.

Chagrined, furious, and still reeling with power, he climbed the nearest tree and launched himself into the sky. He sought an escape from the siren song of her nightmare and needed to be anywhere but here, where the smell mocked his senses and attempted to lure him back onto her chest. He soared over a lake and kept going, using his butterfly form to preserve energy. When he finally reached the outskirts of the city and noticed her scent had become a subdued flavor in the air, he allowed himself to touch down. The rural neighborhood would be enough to distract him with its fields of unyielding crops in the form of ripe young minds. A yellow house with a tall red privacy fence was his first target. The boundary was tall enough to keep away a broad and leggy human, but Traeyr had no problem slinking through a knothole in the wooden board. He allowed the rippling delight to light up his pleasure senses and savored the feeling, reminding himself of the small delights that sustained his existence.

Yes, this is good enough. These small holes are enough, he resigned himself as he forced his way through the lock in the back door.

The home had three suitable hosts for him to feed upon. Two mature and one young and malleable mind. The two women sharing a bed dreamed of the same fear, a fear that plucked at a long-hidden part of Traeyr's essence.

Mothers often dreamed of this nightmare. The first time he'd noticed the trend, it had reminded him of a mother who'd lost her child to a demonic ritual. Since that time, however, he'd grown desensitized and hadn't thought of that woman nor her son in ages, their faces lost to time. He tried to recall her now and instead conjured the muddled faces of centuries of women dreaming the dream she must have lived through all those years ago. The only feature he was certain of were her sharp, pointed ears, the signature mark of a species equally lost to time.

Traeyr stood at the edge of the bed and stared at the worried faces of the mothers, wondering if the woman in his memory also had lines creasing the corners of her eyes. Did she have lines around her lips from laughing? Did she have a crease in her brow from worry?

Ugh! Frustration undulated through his shadows. He grew weaker from the spent energy, wasted on fragile poetry from a lost life. What had snuck its way into his bitter black core that compelled him toward such futile emotions?

He rushed out the seams of the window before he could do something foolish like ease another human's dreams. Especially after he'd already absurdly been caught, he did not want to make this night even worse.

Luckily, this was not his first time in a human inhabitance laid out like this one. Alleyways and paved roads sailed beneath him until he reached a three-story building with individually housed humans less likely to have children. He would feast on their dreams tonight and not allow whatever was in that cursed dreamer's tear to keep him from his fill of nightmares.

A portly man with his hand fully immersed in a bucket of fried chicken lay slack on a stained green couch. His dream was bland and offered nothing of value, but Traeyr perched cross-legged on his chest until the sleeper coughed and turned pale under the weight of him. He sent an explosive burst of power into the sleeper's soul. From his view of the dream, Traeyr watched the corners of the scene blacken until a swirling mist circled the man, who was eating chicken even in his dream. The mist turned all it touched into boiling bubbles of blood. It rushed toward the drumstick the man gnashed in his jaw.

Fear leaked from the sleeper and seeped into Traeyr's power. He left the human there to wallow and moved on to the next. A woman next door who dreamed of her new job. Simply removing her clothing would allot him some power, but the basic anxieties of the overused dream sounded dull and dreary compared to the power he was trying to forget from the alluring dreamer's tear. Instead, he turned her boss into the devil himself with eighteen sets of eyes and a split head, tentacles flowing from the seams of his pressed clothing. Traeyr drank the mortal's nightmare with a smile and licked the familiar taste from his fangs as his semi-corporeal form began to take shape.

The next apartment housed a party of teenagers, all of them dreaming psychedelic dreams. He felt a small twinge of remorse but doused it quickly as he remembered his goal. He would not be made soft by one human woman and her delicious tears. He would be sated.

In this way, he continued through the complex until all of the mortal souls dwelling there were cultivated, though he left each of them with their lives intact. The weight of the door easily gave way under his push as he slung it open and paused on the steps. He stared down at his hands as he flexed them open and shut, then grew a few fleeting butterflies between them. His conjurations danced and twirled between his speckled claws until he put them out with a sizzle.

With this much mass, he would surely be able to feel the woman's touch. It would be the ghost of a feeling, but a sensation all the same.

The thought of her rose unbidden and tugged on an invisible string attached to his nonexistent heart, followed by another curiosity. What was she dreaming about now that he was not there to help?

Some dreams were truly dangerous. They could rise in power and create illnesses of the mind that were not easily cured. The illness perforated the soul of the sleeper, allowing a weakness that was easily exploited by hungry ghosts, demons, and wraiths from to steal the dreamer's body and soul for their own. Modern-day human medicine was ill-equipped to handle such possessions as they lacked the magical touch of the elves and focused too much on the mind of the afflicted. Judging by the strength of her night terrors, the woman was a prime candidate for such an ailment.

Before he realized what he'd talked himself into, Traeyr was dashing through the neighborhood, breezing over the trees, and tangling in the shadows on his way to the mortal's window.

The mellifluous tones of her scent reached him long before he arrived. With a flavorful dulcet of rich tones, it's a wonder the dreamer hadn't been tracked down by a monster more corrupt than Traeyr. Night creatures that dwelled in the domain of terrified sleeping mortals like hags, mares, and incubi, who had been monsters for so long risked losing themselves in the darkness they commanded. It would be simple to do. For a century after the death of his mortal self, Traeyr could have easily succumbed to the darkness. It still called to him on occasion, with whispered promises of a life no longer a slave to consumption, even if it meant a brainless existence. When the whispers became tempting, he knew to remove himself from inhabited places and spend time dwelling in the beauty of the earth.

The woman slept fitfully. The gray sheets bunched in her fists as she thrashed against her innermost horrors. It was a difficult sight to behold. His power thrummed against its borders. He remained powerful even after the energy it took to reach her side so quickly, although his limbs were fading at the tips. He didn't trust himself to ride her chest again this night—nor should he attempt to do so any night now that he knew she was a weakness—

but surely he could ease her suffering from here with a touch more power.

A middle-aged couple with no children or pets slept dreamlessly in the neighboring home. They'd seen many horrors in their day and one more night of dark dreams would do them no great harm. After filling up, he returned to her window and pressed a semi-corporeal hand of flickering shadow to the glass pane.

Her cheeks glistened, little dewy drops of sweet cream that Traeyr balled his fist against the urge to steal for himself. Without riding her, he had no way to consume the slivers of her dream as he shaved them away. but he could send tendrils of shadow to do his bidding. They rose from underneath her bed and left swirling trails in the air as they completed his task.

Once he was satisfied that the intimate details had faded from her private hell into a subdued nightmare, he ripped himself from her window and stalked into the trees.

Chapter 5
Addison

"The night terrors are back again. I had a full-fledged attack of sleep paralysis last night. That hasn't happened since all that stuff with my mom's boyfriend back when I was a teenager."

Addison paced from her bedroom to the living room, walking figure-eights around furniture to keep her restless body moving as she clung to her cell phone. Dr. Ellis lived in Florida, a twenty-minute drive from her old apartment. Going through the new patient process to locate a brand-new therapist and having to re-purge all of her traumas to a total stranger wasn't appealing in the slightest. She'd gone through the grueling process ten times over back home and was grateful she'd come across Dr. Ellis when she had. No way would she do it all again, especially since she planned on moving as soon as her lease allowed. Even if that meant suffering in silence, what was one more year when she'd done exactly that for the majority of her life?

She tilted the phone away from her mouth and tried not to breathe like a maniac on her therapist's voicemail. "Maybe things are worse than I thought. Please give me a call back if you can do a video appointment. Thanks."

Her phone *thunked* onto the couch and promptly slid into the crack behind the cushion. Addison followed it with a shaky sigh, her elbows landing on her knees. Without the obstruction of her phone call, the music clicked on at full volume. She scrambled to locate the device and shut off the music, too wound up to handle it without giving in to the jungle-like feeling of humid anxiety thrumming in the bass.

Nightmares weren't new to her. Quite the opposite. They were one of the most constant things in her life, along with the mountains and valleys of depression that haunted anyone with the heavy weight of past trauma. Night terrors and anxiety loops were like old, reliable friends. It wasn't the presence of bad dreams that worried her. It was the inconsistency of them.

For the past few nights, her dreams had swung from deeply personal past traumas to plain-Jane, movie-esque nightmares that had nothing to do with her at all. The chaotic swing of the pendulum had seemingly no structure whatsoever and reminded her too much of her mom's similar mood swings. Was she grasping at straws, trying to make correlations where there were none? Or could these dreams be a sign of something deeper, something lying dormant in her mind?

To top it off, she'd woken with slickness between her legs each morning. Her preferences and ideas around sex had come up in sessions with Dr. Ellis in the past, who assured her it was normal for people who had experienced abuse to have some confusion around sexuality. Still, it was uncomfortable to think she was turned on by the air of darkness surrounding her dreams, regardless that some were more tame than usual. The only somewhat justifiable explanation for her arousal was the handsome elf whose likeness had emerged in at least two or three of her dreams.

Regardless, she would happily pay Dr. Ellis for another session just to hear her reiterate that Addison was reacting in a reasonable manner.

With her hands still a little shaky, she flipped her palms up and practiced the breathing technique Dr. Ellis had shown her. *Palms up to show my body it's not in danger. Breathe into my belly. Breathe out slowly, as though trying not to douse the flame of a candle.*

At least the calmer nightmares allowed for a reprieve. Not for the first time, she wished she were *normal*. A normal person with normal problems who was afraid of going to work naked.

I'm probably just lonely. She didn't miss Justin's passive-aggressive attitude, but she would give just about anything to be held right now. Hell, she would even hop into the arms of the demonic creature she'd hallucinated while under the spell of sleep paralysis.

That thought made her snort a little and she began to calm down, enough to turn on the music in an attempt to drown out the rest of her panic attack.

Work passed in a blur. Addison had a vague awareness of her body and its surroundings but spent most of the day disassociated or preoccupied with anxiety. Hardly five minutes could go by without feeling the need to check her phone, hoping to find a voicemail from Dr. Ellis, but Addison felt she was doing a decent job of hiding her nerves.

Apparently, she wasn't hiding it well enough, though, because Leah pulled her aside with a concerned look behind her sharp blue eyes.

"Are you okay? I've never seen you this distracted."

"I'm fine." Addison smiled weakly, the lie bringing a quiver to her lips. "Thanks for asking."

She returned to her task, only to have Nasty Nathan wave his hand in front of her face. She raised her gaze to meet his over the dead fish on the counter and bit back a glower at his exaggeratedly dumbfounded expression.

"Earth to Addison!" He snapped his fingers so close to her nose that the action sprayed her with whatever smelly fish fluids coated his thumb and forefinger. He had yet again foregone the plastic gloves he forced them all to wear. "Get your shit together or call someone to come cover for you!"

He stomped away, cursing under his breath.

Addison dug deep and gathered all the scruples she could muster. When she finally made it to her driveway eons later, she stared at her hands on the wheel with the icky blue house blurred in the background.

What is going on with me?

She jumped as the startling sound of her ringtone blared out of her purse in the passenger seat.

"Hello?"

"Hey, Addy, I got your voicemail. How are you doing?"

The woven fabric of the seat covers felt coarse under her fingertips as she used the texture to stay grounded. She gave the summarized version of her recent nightmares and the accompanying sleep paralysis, along with any details of her life as of late that may factor in to her symptoms.

"So, yeah. I don't know. Something's wrong with me." She spoke the last part in jest, but she knew Dr. Ellis was aware of her morbid sense of humor in times like these.

"It's totally natural to feel symptoms of depression and even flashbacks of trauma during times of heightened stress. And no wonder you're stressed with all the bills suddenly your responsibility. Have you been writing in your journal lately?"

Always with the damn journal. She could lie and say she had been, but that would negate the effectiveness of having a therapist. Besides, she knew that journaling and writing things down to process them *did* help her quite a bit. She wasn't sure why it was like pulling teeth to actually do sometimes.

"No. I will."

"Journaling was a great help for you last time you went through a depression. How's your support system? Marissa?"

"I haven't called her in a while. I think I'm feeling too guilty about not having her cover done yet, so I'm scared to talk to her."

"She's been a good friend for you to lean on in the past. Maybe she could provide some excitement for your eventual move back home. You guys could make a mood board for the new place to bring some joy into your day-to-day."

Addison nodded. She absentmindedly brought her index finger to her mouth and chewed on its fingernail.

"You'll get through this, Addy. You're a strong person. Look how far you've come since we last spoke. I'm confident you will get through this, too."

Tears welled in her eyes and she nodded again, knowing Dr. Ellis couldn't see her agreement.

"Let's schedule a session for next week, okay? If anything comes up before then, just give me a call."

Once they settled on a date and she wrote it in the calendar on her phone, they said their goodbyes and hung up. Addison remained in her vehicle and distantly listened to the sound of the motor as she stared at a blank message to Marissa. She wasn't the type of person to call someone out of the blue—that's just rude—so she tried to write a message that conveyed what she needed from her friend.

She was also not the type of person to ask for help, so the words tangled on each other in her mind and never found their way onto the screen.

Preferring to stamp down the emotions her conversation with Dr. Ellis dredged up for later inspection, Addison decided to ditch the sour mood. She blasted her throwback playlist and belted the lyrics to the soundtrack of her angsty teenage years at the top of her lungs, dancing in the shower like she was the star of a hit 2000's music video. She decided this perk of living alone rivaled the ability to toss clothes right into the wash and walk around butt-ass-naked.

When the intrusive thoughts were mostly drowned out and she was out of breath, she pulled up the illustration and zoned out on the details for hours. The streetlight outside her window flickered on sometime during all of this, but she continued to space out on the computer until she couldn't hold her eyes open any longer.

Please let my dreams be better tonight.

Chapter 6
Traeyr

I will not visit her again.

Traeyr recited the pledge repeatedly as the sky turned a dull pink and the moon rose early with its milky white glow. He hunted the surrounding neighborhoods and ignored the reasons why he didn't take his hunt farther away, though brief truths perforated his stubborn wall of denial. The dreamer was vulnerable to evil forces and ill-equipped to handle them. One of those dark forces being her own dreams.

If he were truthful with himself, he would already know he was destined to return to her side this night.

His power stores were replete. Faraway travels were possible with all the nightmarish energy he had saved up, but he found himself wondering what it would be like to use his stored power for something else. Something new.

The thoughts had him staring at his hands again, watching as they plucked a leaf from a red maple tree and twirled the stem between his thumb and forefinger.

The natural world yielded to him, but the amount of sensation that reached his awareness was a faint, insensate version of what could be felt with a real body. The only way he could truly feel the dreamer's touch in all its splendor would be with his mortal form, which could only be conjured by the first half of the binding ritual, the ritual that would trap him in the confines of her bedroom.

Traeyr sneered at the leaf and crushed it in his palm.

An unforgettable scent wafted past him. His eyes drifted closed and he allowed the scent that had dominated his thoughts all day to wash over him. At the tail end of its syrupy sweetness came a musky, earthy smell, like the malodor of an old swamp. The noxious scent invaded his airspace and brought his whole being to attention. He recognized that smell.

Without hesitation, Traeyr condensed his shadows and hastened through the alleys and over the trees. He cursed himself for straying too far, for pretending he could leave her alone and defenseless for any length of time.

A hag lay prostrate on his dreamer's stomach, its brown, decaying, ossified hands wrapped tightly around the woman's neck. It cackled and whispered archaic words, attempting to convince the sleeper to surrender to her deepest fears and concede to the hag's influence. If the dreamer gave in, the hag would possess her body and walk amongst mortals until the possession caused the dreamer's body to rapidly decompose. The creature didn't notice Traeyr's arrival. She cackled and cackled, certain her plan to corrupt the mortal and steal her body and soul was indisputable.

Traeyr forced his way through a slit in the wall and sent a potent wave of shadows to knock the hag off balance. She fell to the clattered to the ground in pile of bones.

The blast was not enough to rid them of her, though, and her skeletal remains picked themselves up one by one until she paced the room, dragging a long, crooked fingernail against the wall.

The sleeping form opened her dark eyes as Traeyr stood above her defensively. He had to stand his ground or the hag would use dark magic to steal her from his grasp. He cast a woeful glance down at the woman and rushed a force of sleep magic into her through the soles of his feet upon her chest.

"You dare challenge me? I was here before your kind drew upon the shadows!"

The hag's voice was jarring, her words harsh like the sound of rough stones scraping against each other. Traeyr ignored her and siphoned the shadows from every corner and crevice of the home, drawing on the deepest stores of power within himself until a great tsunami wave of blackness rose behind the hag. It crashed over her and flooded the room. Traeyr sank to the bed and grasped the sheets around the sleeping woman's form protectively.

He vaguely felt the woman clawing at the edge of his induced sleep. When the last of the shade dribbled out the window, he glanced down to check on her well-being.

Tears glistened in the V-shaped lines on her temples. Sweat beaded at her widow's peak. Traeyr focused his waning power into the tip of one claw so that it held steady, then traced the heart-shaped line of her face and brought the claw to his lips. The moisture tasted ambrosial, but a faint trace of vinegar alerted him to the human's worsening condition. The hag had left her mark on the woman's already darkening dreams.

Another lick of her wet cheek had his form nearly substantial again already, and this time the dreamer's fluids gave him an unexpected taste of her determination, her resilience through unimaginable pain.

The dreamer's eyelids peeled apart heavily and locked onto him.

For a brief moment, Traeyr stared back. He wondered if she thought he was the cause of her suffering. Wondered if she would believe that he wasn't. Wondered if her liquid tasted differently when offered to him freely.

Chapter 7
Addison

Her plea for a good night's sleep went unanswered for a long time. All-consuming nightmares dragged her into the depths of the blackest corners of her mind. The walls rising in her nightmare were full of demonic faces. Everywhere she looked was blight and evil. The piece of her that remained lucid curled itself into a ball and waited for the night to end.

At some point, she woke up, unable to move. A thin, dirty woman with eyes glowing bright red and matted hair falling in patches from her scalp scraped a long fingernail across Addison's skin. The hallucination let out a shrill laugh, the strident sound grating her eardrums.

The creature crawled onto the end of the bed and crept up on spindly, spider-like limbs until its weight held her down.

Addison's eyes darted around the room helplessly. She begged for it to end but couldn't use her voice.

The realm of sleep beckoned her again and the sound of fuzzy white noise like a forgotten television set invaded her senses. The final thing she saw before falling under was a pair of yellow-orange eyes set against soft black fur.

The dream she returned to was not a pleasant one, but she settled into a long pace, attempting to outrun whatever was chasing her. It wasn't the chase that scared her, but some nagging part of her mind was determined to check on her bodily safety in the waking world. She tried to claw her way free of the dream to confront the monsters in her bedroom.

After many failed attempts, she breached the veneer of sleep. Unable to move under an overbearing weight on her chest, she tried to scream but choked. Yellow-orange eyes glowed as they regarded her.

Then it was over. As soon as she awoke, the sleep paralysis fiend vanished in a wave of shadows and her voice returned, her own scream startling her.

Her hands flew to her mouth as she scrambled backwards in bed. The demon's receding form transformed into a butterfly, and then he was gone.

What the hell was that?!

Addison had no doubt what she'd seen was real. A shadow in the shape of a fur-covered man with two swirling horns and bright glowing eyes perched on her chest.

The only light seeping through the uncovered window was the streetlight. Addison snatched her phone from the bedside table. Four-thirty. There was no way she could fall back asleep now. She threw off the covers and shivered, pulled on the gray sweatpants she'd hastily discarded at the foot of the bed, and slunk into the computer chair.

Maybe some obscure online forum would know what the ghostly form had been. Heart racing, she tried to recall more details, conjuring to mind the look of deep curiosity she'd woken to. He had stared down at her in wonder with an expression that almost seemed affectionate. *That can't be right. I'm losing my mind.*

Her trembling fingers fumbled at the keyboard. The first search brought up information on incubi, but he hadn't been doing something naughty with her sleeping body—right? No, he'd looked protective and even contrite.

Her next keywords brought up pages about night hags. *Wait a moment.* An image of a painting depicting a night hag jarred her memory. There had been a woman of this description in her room, too. A gross, dirty skeleton with mangy hair covered in mud. A shiver chased up her spine as she recalled the feel of a long fingernail against her skin.

Could the furry demon have been protecting her against the night hag?

The third search was a gold mine. A demon with many names around the world, including mara, mare, alp, maere; according to legend, these sleep paralysis demons inspired the term nightmare. They rode their victim's chest in their sleep, rendering the person unable to move, breathe, or cry out, and sometimes crushing them to death. They took pleasure in locating the smallest hole to infiltrate a sleeping human's bedroom, licked their hair, and ate the fear from the nightmares they fed their victims.

This explained her recent bout of sleep paralysis. She'd bothered Dr. Ellis for nothing. Great! Just what she needed—demons feuding over who got to give her the worst dreams.

Reading further, she found a handful of accounts where people trapped the mara in its human form. Apparently, these demons were usually female. Not surprisingly, some medieval douchebags trapped the thing and then married it. A free wife.

This one had definitely *not* been female. A weird thrill ran up her spine as she recalled his male...*equipment* on her chest.

The website went on to provide ways to repel a mara. They all sounded ridiculous, like something they might've told children back in the olden days to get them to sleep. Put your shoes next to the bed facing the door. Place your thumb in your hand. Cross your arms and legs before you fall asleep. Something about severed horse heads.

Fresh out of horse heads, Addison came up with a hodgepodge plan based on far-fetched legends. She would wait until she felt his presence on her chest and then call out to the demon, claiming he could borrow something from her in the morning. According to the tales, it would be spellbound to leave and return in the light of dawn to collect.

Then what? I ask it nicely to leave me the hell alone?

Knowing her track record with confrontations, she reread the whole article for a solution that didn't require her to stare down a demon with a confidence she didn't possess. Perhaps she could cross her limbs and try to fall asleep that way. It didn't sound very comfortable, though, and what about the night hag? Would it return?

Last time she'd seen the furry demon, she'd had semi-decent nightmares, despite waking unable to move. In fact, she'd even noticed the shadow-cloaked butterfly the night before that, the first night her usual terrors had been sporadically replaced with lesser ones.

It became increasingly apparent that he was not the problem, which rose another question in her mind. Was he the source of her arousal? It couldn't be ironic that the term was *ridden by a mare* and she was waking up slick with desire. The term was innately sexual. Right?

Oh, god. He must have been the little shadow wisp that watched her masturbate.

She should feel violated right now. So why did she have the urge to go rub one out?

Her alarm blared from the nightstand. *Shit!* She had to get ready for work and deal with all of this nonsense later.

Chapter 8
Traeyr

After the close call with the night hag, Traeyr ceded to the possessive half of himself, which he'd been trying and failing to ignore. He spent the day strategizing a way to alert the dreamer to her condition. If he could get her to see the situation for what it was and seek help, perhaps he could wash his hands of her and finally leave this land.

A door slammed. Traeyr hid amongst the shadows under her bed. He peered up at the peculiar woman who'd captured his interest and wondered why she looked as conflicted as he felt. He nearly blew his cover and ran to her to influence her body to lie down so he could fuel himself with her liquid and suck on her dreams, to bring her a sense of comfort and ease the worried lines on her forehead.

Was it possible she remembered him from the night before? Did she think he'd caused her harm and searched for the knowledge to cast him out? It would be better if she did, he decided, for he realized he would never again be able to keep himself from her chest. Not with the tantalizing scent wafting from every crack and hole in her home and not with all the creatures that scent attracted.

His wild streak of selfishness surprised him. He had never felt so possessive of a dreamer before.

Patience was another trait he was not accustomed to. The only thing that kept him from using his influence on her was the fragment of fear that she would recognize his butterfly. He grew weaker as time passed to the beat of deafening music, but he remained hidden until finally she silenced the room, shed her trousers, and climbed into bed.

An intoxicating thrill rippled through him as he waited for her sleeping mind to call to him with its addictive scent.

It took a little while before her fragrant mind drifted through the air, and when it did, it was barely a whisper. Even that tiny hint of the delicious aroma sent shivers through Traeyr. He greedily rose from his hiding place to hover above her chest.

He'd barely settled onto her breast when her eyes snapped open.

"Mara, return in the morning and I will lend you something!"

The air turned into a vacuum. Traeyr's disembodied shadows whipped and swirled painfully as he was sucked through the crack of her window in disorganized gusts. Ancient magic forcefully banished him from the room, leaving his mind reeling from the sting of betrayal.

Witch!

The ungrateful mortal! Tendrils of shadows lagged behind the rest of him. With a painful lump in his chest, he denounced the emotions he'd attached to his one-sided companionship.

It was always fated to be this way.

The thought did not reassure him, but he stomped to the beat of it anyway. This was what happened when humans got the best of his kind. They took advantage, used his gifts, and discarded the rest of him like garbage. He knew he had no right to feel so betrayed, but her banishment stung in a way he couldn't have imagined. He hardened the unwanted emotion to ice and coated himself in a protective shield.

How did she find that trick? Humans had long forgotten how to weild the magic in words, hidden under false messages and distracted by their fancy tools and technologies. Had she found a fae folk to tell of his secrets?

He cursed her all the way from her house to the edge of a nearby wood. The shadows recoiled from his wrath. Inside the cover of the trees, he roared his fury into the deep.

A melodic tone of smells teased his senses. Even from this distance, he could detect her unique scent. The bouquet of flavors was laced with fear, anguish, sorrow, and strife. Foolish mortal! She would not be suffering if she hadn't sent him away.

Her ignorance mixed with his ire. Soon he found himself traipsing back to civilization, his limbs moving of their own accord. He fed on unsuspecting sleepers and channeled his anger into his craft, reaping and sewing nightmares with flourishing intensity.

The nightmares fueled him but did nothing to ease the ache inside his empty soul. Worry for the woman threatened his control and forced him to continue through the night, swallowing tasteless dreams whole. What he was about to do would take a great deal of power, and there was a chance it would be morning before he acquired enough.

Many torturous hours later, with her repellent charm at its thinnest in her deep sleep, he sidled up to the window. A tendril of his power seeped through the crack. He bid the shadows to rise from under her bed and settle on her chest.

Just enough to ease her anguish. Nothing more.

Foolish dreamer. She may have forced him away for the night, but at the first light of morning, he would be pulled just as roughly into her chambers to collect the debt.

He knew exactly what he would demand.

Chapter 9
Addison

Unabated attacks of horror-filled dreams tormented Addison all night. Scenes from her past mixed with nail-biting anxieties, creating dramatized memories that twisted into untold evil. Her family was murdered, only to be reborn determined to seek vengeance on her. Abusers resurfaced wearing new faces like that of her greasy boss. The relentless onslaught had her waking in sweats, thrashing about like a fish out of water, only to be thrown upon the gutting table.

After what felt like ages, Addison's lucid mind picked up on an incoming respite. A dark hallway with no light, but also no haunting ghosts or writhing demons. A torch leaned in its sconce. She retrieved it and held it at arm's length.

In the corner of her vision, a wavering figure caught the light. The handsome elf flickered like a mirage before disappearing altogether.

The simple dream eased her into wakefulness. It was still dark outside the window, but she decided not to risk going back to sleep. She'd be happy never returning to that hellscape ever again.

To her exasperation, she found her panties slick, albeit nothing like they'd been in nights prior. With a quick peek around the room, she shed the soft black fabric and dropped them in the washer.

She searched her dresser for a fresh pair of underwear and realized she'd been filling the washer without actually running any loads. After sniff-checking and discarding her worn sweatpants, she'd barely pulled on a pair of black leggings when dark shadows poured in through the cracks of her window and materialized into an the vague shape of a body.

The tips of two horns swirled upward but dissolved into flickering shadows before reaching their points. The silhouette looked fuzzy, just a collection of billowing haze. His torso was lean and cut but looked more smooth than the rest of him. Her eyes trailed lower to where his male bits were, and she felt a pang of gratitude and disappointment when she saw the contour merely gave way to penumbra.

Even with the deep glower etched in the writhing pall of his face, the sight of him made her inner walls clench with excitement.

As though he sensed her lust, his cheek rose in a wolfish grin. His narrowed gaze flicked down to her thighs, a black tongue flicking out to graze the lip above a sharp tooth.

"What are you?" She commended herself for standing her ground, though her voice shook with the strain of confrontation.

His haughty grin soured back into a sneer as he bared his teeth at her. Two sharp canines hung over his bottom lip as he growled, the sound deep and rumbling and reminiscent of a wild bear.

"You don't know what magic you dabble in, human."

The intensity of his gaze sharpened. Addy leaned back on the desk and pressed her thighs together, trying and failing to keep her mind on the task at hand. She was supposed to be interrogating him, not wondering what his fangs would feel like scraping up her inner thigh, or whether his shadows would have enough mass to hold her immobile against the bed while he ravaged her.

At least the dirty thoughts made it easier not to be afraid of the conversation at hand. Instead of worrying over the confrontation, her body pulsed with a growing sense of emptiness, as though she suddenly direly needed to be filled.

His nostrils flared again and she realized it was not a coincidence. She had no doubt he could smell the struggle she was losing with her body. *Oh well. It doesn't change what I have to do.*

"Are you the reason I've been having night terrors again? Waking up unable to move?" She admired herself for keeping a steady voice despite her distracting desire. Shadows swelled around him. Her comment seemed to bristle him. She braced against the desk and prepared for retaliation, but his rippling edges smoothed and he began to pace. His vague silhouette surged with nebulous mist throughout his limbs, never fully forming but always moving. He stalked to her bed and stared down at the unmade sheets, his claw-tipped hands clasped behind his back.

"You do realize I decide what you lend me."

She hadn't realized that, but it didn't change anything. What could he possibly want from her? "Answer my questions first."

He stilled. His chin tilted in her direction as another wave of bristling darkness crossed over his boundless form.

Her pluck surprised her as much as it clearly did him. *Good.* On paper, he had the upper hand right now, being a demon and all. Not to mention the throwing her off-kilter. He could use a bit of a curveball, too.

Silently, he crossed the room, unhindered by the bed in his way. As he walked-slash-floated toward her, he grew in height until he towered over her, his darkness cloaking her vision in shade.

"I am a mahr. I am the sole reason for the human term nightmare."

"Why were you on top of me?"

He cocked a dark brow and a slow, predatory grin graced his lips. "You smelled good."

"So you gave me nightmares? That seems unfair."

"I don't play by your human rules. I could have done much worse. By the taste of you, I know you're riddled with terrors." His looming form receded and she could practically see him wrestling to regain his aloof persona. "Perhaps I should have let the hag take you as its host. They like the broken ones the best."

Addison pushed away the sting of his words and focused on her goal. Whether he'd meant to or not, he'd just revealed vital information.

"Then you were behind the boring nightmares." An idea blossomed. "Could you give me good dreams?"

"I was." His stoicism was back in full force. He leaned against the washing machine across the hall, though she figured it was all an act since she'd witnessed him walk through the bed like it wasn't even there. "But I will not make the same mistakes of my past. You are in no place to make demands, mortal."

Something about the way he called her mortal sent liquid heat through her core again, but she persisted. She stood straight and rolled her shoulders back.

"What do you want to borrow? I'm sure we can make a deal."

"No." His voice boomed like a sudden clap of thunder. The shadowy tips of his form raced outward in a burst of harsh black, then softened back into the wispy demonic body. "I will be trapped by no mortal."

Addison rolled her eyes. "I don't want to trap you, dude. I just want a good night's sleep. I haven't slept very well since... Well, I'm not great at sleeping alone."

The mahr's consuming gaze flayed her alive. Long moments of silence stretched between them while his expression gave no indication of his thoughts. Her heart raced. She was about to press him for an answer when he straightened and gave her another sultry grin.

"One night. One dream."

"Thank you!" She almost leaped into his arms but caught herself, which seemed to amuse him.

"Don't thank me yet," he said and pressed his tongue to the tip of his sharp tooth. He glanced between her thighs again.

"Right. What do you want to borrow?" His eyes lingered on her sex. When he lifted them to hers, they were heavily lidded with blatantly wanton thoughts. "The fabric that was between your legs last night."

Addison's brows threatened to fly from her forehead even as another surge of liquid heat flew to her cunt. The mahr watched her reaction with satisfaction written in every wisp and flicker of his being. He leaned forward and exaggeratedly dragged in a deep breath, his eyelids fluttering in a way that had nothing to do with his unusual form.

"You want my *panties*?"

His grin deepened.

It doesn't change anything. So he wants me, too. Maybe I can use that to my advantage. She didn't have to pretend as she settled into the decision. She licked her lips, watching as his heady gaze tracked her every movement. Summoning every ounce of fierce sexuality she could muster, she sauntered to the laundry closet and leaned over the rim, letting her ass stick in the air a little higher and a little longer than necessary. She could feel him studying her body and wondered what filthy thoughts were going through his mind, wondered if they matched the fantasies weaving through her own.

She didn't even know if he was able to touch her, to truly touch her, let alone fill her. Surely if he were fantasizing about it, that meant he had his ways, right?

"Here. Keep them."

The mahr accepted her offering and brought the damp red cloth to his face, promptly dragging in a deep breath. Her clit pulsed with deep-rooted need and then a surge of wetness flooded her as he slipped out his tongue and licked the fabric. His previously undefined edges gorged with power, every inch of him appearing solid.

Her jaw dropped as she took in this version of him. At least eight feet tall, with broad shoulders covered in fur and an abdomen wired with muscle, he was certainly strong enough to rip her in half without even having to use his fangs. She instinctively glanced down—though it was more like eye level now—and was rewarded with the glorious sight of his thick cock. Even only half-erect, he was way larger than anything she'd taken before. A frisson of fear chased by delight rose from her core and skittered up her spine.

"Oh, god," she breathed.

His libidinous gaze blazed into her soul. "There is no god here. I'll see you tonight, dreamer."

"Wait!" She fumbled for something to say as she leaned against the washer for support, clenching her knees together. "My name's Addison. What's yours?"

His growl was violent and held none of his previous lust. "I'll not be fooled so easily. Until tonight, *Addison*."

Chapter 10
Traeyr

Proof of the human's desire thrilled Traeyr.

Her pheromones played his senses like instruments lost to time, the sweet scent held notes like elven harps and organs he'd long forgotten. What was it about this human that had him so sentimental? She'd crossed her arms over her abundant chest, no doubt to be defiant, which had made the ample swell of her breast even more enticing. The image of her plump behind teased his memory. The black cloth hiding her flesh had clung to the secret mound between her legs and when she'd leaned over the machine, a breeze of mouth-watering smells assaulted him in the best way. He fantasized about ripping the fabric away and devouring the source of the delectable scent until she begged for release, using his shadows to hold her still.

Those filthy thoughts led to another, more ridiculous notion. What would her flesh feel like against his? His imagination ran rampant, filling in the blanks where he would never have the answer. The unattainable sensation was pointless to consider. He refused to be bound to a mortal, refused to do anyone's bidding, but still he wondered how it would feel to enact the binding ritual with her. To ride her bountiful chest with his own flesh and bone body. The image of her beneath him, maple syrup brown eyes locked on his, mouth hanging open, nails digging into his thighs. It sent shivers through him at the thought of such a forbidden act.

His magic shouldn't be capable of inciting such a strong reaction in her body, requiring her to shed her underclothes each morning. Then again, he'd never found himself in this position before, and his own body was behaving unnaturally, too. Perhaps it was natural for his comforting touch of magic to thrill a human female—if one could consider his docile nightmares comforting, which was another concern. She was unaware of how detrimental her night terrors were to her health, nor what creatures of the night were set on stealing her soul.

The day stretched on with his mind consumed by thoughts of the dreamer and all her tight holes he longed to fill. He couldn't shake the throbbing sense of need that welled within him, but he thrust it away to focus on feeding. He must fill up on sleepers to ensure he had enough power to take form when he arrived in her chambers. Her dreams would sustain him once she slept, but he wanted to be ready the moment they met. After every handful of sleepers, he meandered back to the tree where he'd stashed her panties and braced himself for the rush of addictive power that crashed over him each time he licked her sweet sap.

Twilight's deep glow graced the sky by the time he felt adequately nourished. The shadows clung to their master as he made his way back to her home.

A foreign vehicle was parked in her driveway. Traeyr bristled and watched as a human male strode confidently to the front door. He inserted a key into the aperture that Traeyr was coming to think of fondly. It clicked and gave way to the stranger, which sent another wave of irritation through Traeyr.

Carefully clutching his power as tightly condensed as possible, Traeyr followed the man inside. He remained out of sight as the man pulled one of humankind's most prevalent devices from his pocket and busied himself with it while he spun circles in Addison's chair.

"Hey, babe. I know we haven't been talking lately, but call me back."

Traeyr growled at the term of endearment. The oblivious male kicked out of his boots and shrugged off a light jacket, then languidly spread out on Addison's bed.

Traeyr waited impatiently for the man to fall asleep. The moment he heard snores, he zipped out of the shadows and perched on the man's chest.

Addison was under no obligation to disclose a mate. She was free to take as many mates as she liked, even a deeply devoted partnership with whomever she pleased. Traeyr knew that. Despite her sexual desire for him, the companionship he felt toward her was one-sided, and even that was entirely made up in his overly active imagination. What he felt for her was more about her smell—well, and her taste—than about her as a woman.

Even so, he found himself staring at the male with a deep aversion bordering on hatred. As with many of his feelings as of late, hatred was an unusual one; he didn't even hate the man who turned him into a demon, not anymore. His bitterness toward the man who'd cursed him had dispelled after beholding the wonders of this magnificent earth ten times over.

But this human lying in *her* bed, complicating his plans tonight, calling her human terms of endearment, elicited strong emotions.

If it turned out this man was one of Addison's mates, she would surely be angry at him for what he was about to do. Without hesitation, Traeyr reached for the man's dreams and gave them a good solid spin, sending the man pirouetting through a ballroom of horrors while Traeyr smirked down spitefully.

Have I not seen this man before? Traeyr took a moment to study the man's high cheekbones and broad forehead, his crooked nose and thick eyebrows, and realized he had seen this face before—in the spillover from one of Addison's dreams. Except, in the clipped images from her nightmare, this man was acting out a role from Addison's childhood.

Nightmares often switched the faces of villains from a person's memory, along with other bits of information that the nightmare deemed interchangeable. When pain from the present reminded the subconscious mind of a pain from their history, nightmares eagerly used that as fuel. Nightmares could be cruel acts of punishment that served as warnings or persuasion to the subconscious to build more walls around the person's soul. Traeyr knew of this mechanism of the sleeping mind, but humans often discarded it, not realizing that they had little choice in the way their subconscious implemented these subliminal messages.

Knowing this man had hurt his dreamer deeply enough to affect her in this way made it difficult for Traeyr not to break the man's bones.

He could.

He could easily press his full weight down upon the human male, crushing the bones that encased his heart and lungs until they were fodder around punctured and useless organs. Then he would never hurt Addison again. Would never cause pain, be it physical or emotional, to the dreamer Traeyr had become entirely too possessive of.

Choked breaths forced their way from the man's throat. Traeyr watched him struggle, felt him clawing for breath in the dream as his bones were depressed under Traeyr's weight in the bedroom. His bones bent with the pressure, so close to snapping that his pale features turned gray, his breathing inconsistent. As tempting as it was, it would not remove the damage already done to Addison. It would only cause more trauma when she came home to a dead lover's body in her bed. Traeyr eased off.

The man beneath him ground his teeth against the nightmares Traeyr fed him. Traeyr watched with a bored expression, his gaze drifting over his shoulder every so often to watch for the door. He wondered what Addison would do with this unexpected visit from her past, but mostly, he wondered how long it would take for this man to leave so he could be alone with the dreamer he couldn't keep out of his mind.

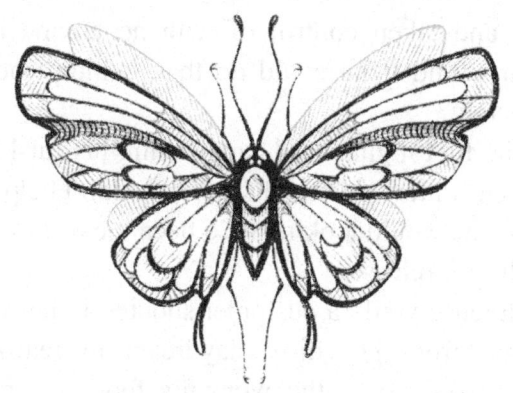

Chapter 11
Addison

Leah gave Addison a dark look from the trout counter the moment she walked in. Nasty Nathan must be in one of his moods. Addison's lip threatened to curl in disgust. She pushed away the ever-present regret, the shame she felt about having gone to school for years just to wind up working for a creep like him in a stinky dump like this.

Thoughts about the bright-eyed demon stayed just out of reach as she went through the motions. Conflicting ideas tugged at her. She felt like a cliché cartoon speaking to an angel and demon on either shoulder. No matter how hard she tried, she couldn't focus on any task put in front of her. Her mind stayed in the gutter, wondering what kind of magic tricks he had up his sleeve. Could he control the shadows? What could he do with them? She'd always been curious about being bound, tied down, and taken control of with no escape from the pleasure. And if he could do that, couldn't he fill her completely?

The first night she'd caught him, his fur-lined face had been contorted with bliss. She couldn't help wondering how he would look if she'd been the one to give him that blissful release.

"Excuse you!" a customer shouted in her face. She emerged from her dirty daydream to realize she'd clomped right over the woman's foot. She rushed to course-correct and wound up spilling the entire contents of her sample tray down the woman's back.

"Oh my—I'm so sorry!"

"Manager! Manager! MANAGER!" the woman shrieked, her face turning brighter than a red snapper bass.

Fantastic. Addison rushed behind the counter and knocked on Nasty Nathan's door. He opened it and pushed her aside, the angry sneer in his eyes hiding behind a plastered smile meant only for the customers to see.

I've got to do something about this. She couldn't work while she was this hot and bothered, not with the dinner rush in full swing. She stepped into Nathan's office and slammed the door behind her. The heavy wooden door held her weight as she leaned back and unbuttoned her slacks. She removed her plastic gloves and shoved a hand unceremoniously down her pants. She slid her fingers under the soft fabric of her panties and dragged them through her slick folds.

She pictured the horned man looming above her, this time situated between her thighs. His horns twisted into fathomless shadows and his face contorted with bliss while he pumped into her. Would his thick cock fit inside her? Surely if it did, she would be able to see it form a lump in her stomach with each thrust while she was immobilized, stuck to the bed and forced to watch him use her body like a sex doll. She remembered the way he'd greedily licked the wet streak on her discarded panties. His eyes had rolled back in their dark lids, like her fluid was a dessert that he had to have in order to live.

Oh, god, yes, yes.

She rode her fingers and quickened the circles on her taut nub until she came undone. She released the breath that felt like she'd been holding ever since he left her room that morning.

The doorknob rustled, then jiggled more intensely as Nasty Nathan started to bang on the door.

"Who the fuck is in there? Open up!"

She hastily buttoned her pants and stepped away from the door. Nathan barged in, nearly falling flat on his face. "What are you doing in here? Get out! Get out! Go back to work!"

"Yes, sir," she mumbled.

The dinner rush flew by with her mind a little more clear. Once there was a solid fifteen minutes between customers, Addison decided she wasn't really needed anymore and had better places to be—like in bed with a horned demon riding her chest.

"Hey, Leah, can you cover my closing chores if I leave early?" "Totally, but good luck getting Nate's permission to leave. He's in a mood."

"When isn't he?" It didn't matter. She would lie to him if she had to.

A soft rap on the door was all it took for Nathan to yell out at her, but she couldn't tell what he was saying. She creaked the door open. His boots were kicked up on the table, the top button of his jeans undone, his hairy belly protruding over the waistline.

Ugh, I could have done without that image my whole life.

"Nate, I really need to leave early. I'm—"

"Are you serious, Trish? It's an employee! I swear to god! I can't keep firing people just because you—Trish!" His shout took her by surprise and only then did she realize he was on the phone. He held the phone away from his ear and glowered at her. "Whatever, Addy, go! I don't give a shit!"

Oookay, then. She backed away slowly and shut the door. "Well, that works."

With a wave in Leah's direction, she rushed out the door and sprinted to her car. It was only seven o'clock, so it was unlikely she would fall asleep as soon as she got home, but still she sped on the highway.

She was excited about a good night's sleep. That's all. Even just one dream that wasn't frightening. One nice, relaxing, peaceful dream like normal people had—that would be enough to drastically improve her morning.

But in her heart—and other parts of her body—she knew the excitement didn't end there.

Chapter 12
Addison

A familiar green truck was parked in her driveway. Her heart hammered, all of the earlier excitement transmuting into anxiety. Her palms slicked against the steering wheel. She took a few deep breaths before parking beside the curb, not wanting to block Justin's path. No way was she going to let him sneak back into her life, not after ditching her with the bills and one measly text message.

She reached for her phone with shaky hands. She wasn't afraid of Justin, but she hated confrontation. How had he even gotten inside? Apparently, the leasing office had given him the spare key, having seen him tour the house with her. *Is that even legal? He's not on the lease!*

One missed voicemail. From Justin.

"Hey, babe. I know we haven't been talking lately, but call me back."

"What the fuck!" she screamed and threw her phone on the floor of the passenger seat.

Great timing, asshole. If she hadn't just made a tentative deal with a demon—a fine-as-hell demon—she may have fallen for his manipulative bullshit. If it were three, maybe four days prior, she would have gladly turned a blind eye to his gaslighting, if only to have a warm body in her bed at night and a distraction from her self-sabotaging thoughts. Loud music did wonders to keep the thoughts at bay, but it was no replacement for human interaction. Even if that interaction was forced and basically make-believe, at least it was tangible.

Now, however, she had more important things to do. She nearly tripped on her way out of the car and slammed the door behind her. She allowed her anxiety over the impending confrontation to encourage her fury. Anger was a useful tool. It could be wielded and used to take action. Just like Dr. Ellis had said, right? *Feel your feelings.*

Well, she was certainly feeling something.

Justin sat on the edge of the bed she had bought for herself with his head in his hands. He looked pathetic. He barely lifted his chin to look at her until she leaned into his eye line, arms clutched around her chest and brows high and demanding.

"*'Hey, baby?'* What the ever-loving fuck, Justin? You have got to be kidding me!"

Justin stood and moved toward her as though about to wrap her in his arms. She shot her hands out and snapped his wrists away from her. He looked surprised.

Did he expect me to fall back into his arms? The answer was obvious, but what stung the most was the truth in it. She would have. She would have taken one look at his face, seen his intent, and said, *you don't even have to apologize. Can we pretend this never happened and move on?* Because she was nothing if not a master of avoidance.

"Look, Addy. I'm sorry. I should have talked to you about how I was feeling." He threw his hands up and then slumped down into her computer chair. "I'm sorry. I shouldn't have up and left like that."

"You think?"

"I mean, I *did* try to tell you—"

"Stop right there, buster. None of this matters. You left me here with all the bills, knowing I couldn't pay them and look for a new job at the same time."

"I didn't mean to hurt you."

She gaped at him. Angry red bumps raised the hair on her arms and climbed the back of her neck. So unaccustomed to voicing her feelings and articulating the thoughts inside her head while clouded with anger, hurt, and betrayal, she sputtered as she tried to clobber together a sentence. Laughter bubbled up inside her as her emotions tangled, the conflicting signals from her body sending mixed messages to the part of her brain in charge of emotion regulation. If she weren't so caught up in this moment, she would think of all the tools Dr. Ellis had tried—and obviously failed—to implement in her life.

Laughter won. She doubled over in a fit of giggles that was definitely *not* what she needed right now, but at least it was better than tears.

"Justin…you dumb fucking…fuck. Get the…fuck…out of…my…house!" The whole sentence took her minutes to form around the hiccupping laughter that ripped through her airway.

"What are you laughing at? Are you laughing at me? I'm trying to have a serious conversation about our relationship!"

"I'm not…trying…to laugh." But she couldn't stop. "Leave! There…is no…relationship!"

Justin stood from the chair so quickly that it toppled over, knocking into the desk hard enough to make everything shake. Stevie tipped over and her wish jar rolled onto the floor, stopped only by the toe of her shoe.

"Whatever, dude. You're a bitch."

That made her laugh even harder, a real laugh this time. She lowered onto the bed so she could clutch her aching tummy and double over at the waist. Tears sprang from her eyes, but she wasn't sure if they were from laughing so hard or if they were the tears that usually showed up when faced with conflict. *A little late.*

The front door slammed shut. Addison wrestled for control of her emotions. She held out her arms and watched her fingers shake as she choked down the laughter and breathed. *Palms up to show my body it's not in danger. Breathe into my belly. Breathe out slowly, as though trying not to extinguish a candle.*

When her breathing and shaking were under control, she realized what she'd just done.

She stood up for herself.

Maybe Dr. Ellis didn't do so bad after all. Sure, there had been way more laughter involved than she expected, and she hadn't been able to voice how much he'd hurt her. But she kicked him out. She didn't let him back into her life simply because he showed up and expressed a willingness to go back to their safe little lie, their act of pretend that made her feel needed.

She made a mental note to tell Dr. Ellis about it when they spoke next week, then took a final deep breath and slipped into the bathroom for her post-work shower. Right before stepping in, she realized there was no towel on the rack and went back into the bedroom to find one.

The mahr's little black butterfly danced around her room.

Chapter 13
Addison

He flitted from one surface to the next as she searched for the box of extra towels. Her heart fluttered like the tips of his wings and she gave him a pointed look before returning to the shower.

The warm water tickled her skin as it gained pressure. The images of her daydreams at work resurfaced as she watched the doorknob, hoping he would squeeze through the hole and wondering if it truly felt good to him. The website said these demons found great pleasure in a tight squeeze and that was why they sought out the smallest holes to infiltrate their victims' houses and bedrooms. The thought of his pleasure at *tight holes* made her inner walls flutter at the same time as a new insecurity blossomed. Would he find her holes tight enough?

When a tendril of shadow slipped through the closed door, she closed her eyes and pinched her nipples until they were taut enough to cut glass. She soaped her hands and rubbed under her heavy breasts provocatively. It wasn't lost on her that the demon who'd taken an interest in her had a thing for boobs. Luckily for him, her body type meant she had a busty chest, and while it had been a source of insecurity at times, she gladly embraced the trait right now.

She leaned her head against the wall. She wanted to touch herself, but she didn't want to give him that satisfaction—not yet. She wanted him to take that for himself, wanted him to *need* to fill her as much as she needed him to quell the growing emptiness within her.

After the shower, she felt wound tight as a ball of rubber bands. If only one piece was let loose, the whole thing would crumble and she would melt into a pile of rubber goo from the heat of her desire. She had no idea how she would ever get to sleep like this, but then the shadowy insect perched on her chest. Suddenly she felt exhausted, her whole body heavy, like a boulder dropped in the ocean. As if in a trance, she crossed to her bed and lay down wearing only her towel.

The mahr's shadow-tipped and frayed edges expanded into a compact version of his demonic form no more than five feet tall, with some body parts less defined than others. He splayed his legs over her to straddle her chest, the undefined edges of his legs leaving a lot to the imagination. She watched with wide eyes, confounded by the way his weight hardly touched her. Her mouth dropped open in amazement.

"That's not necessary," he teased with a predatory grin. He reached down and closed her jaw, pressing a thumb to the seam of her lips.

Through her exhaustion, she felt her core blaze with that peek into what was going through his mind. *Is it always sexual for him?* Did he feel this way about all his victims?

What did she care if he did?

Before she had time to consider the answers to those preposterous questions, a beautiful dream began to unfold around her.

A sea of lush green blanketed the ground from her eagle-eyed view as they soared through the sky. The densely textured flora rose and fell, then split in the middle to frame a sun-dappled body of water surrounded on either side by mountains. The peaks of the mountains inclined higher than her view, rising out of sight in the cloud-flecked sky.

Addison reveled in the magnificent vision. Would she ever see something this beautiful again? It was almost heartbreaking to think this would be the only time she experienced this kind of dream. She struggled to stay in the moment.

A plain white butterfly glided through the air beside her. She recognized it as the mahr and rolled to the side, her dream body easily cutting through the air as if she were weightless. The butterfly settled onto her finger as the landscape gently rose to meet them. A field of lavender greeted her, so soft it could've been a bed of clouds. She rolled onto her back and laughed. Her mind was so free here, like all the things she usually carried weighed no more than the butterfly's wing. What she wouldn't give to stay here, in this moment, utterly free from her thoughts.

The mahr perched on a stalk of lavender, dipping it with his weight to tickle her nose. She laughed and reached for him, but instead of settling on her finger, the butterfly multiplied until a swarm of little white butterflies skittered over her body. Their little legs and fluttering wings tickled through the dainty fabric of the old-fashioned nightgown she was adorned in.

Distantly, she felt pressure on her sleeping chest. The mahr was riding her in the real world, and while she didn't know what all that really entailed, the thought was enough to send a rush of desire to her cunt. Her back arched in response to her body's rising need. The mahr must have understood what was building within her because his swarm of butterflies collected into another form.

This time, he was not just a shadowy outline. He had a real body, covered in jet-black fur with a soft, velvet-padded abdomen, curved horns, slender lips, and fanged teeth that sent shivers through her as he dragged them across her neck.

"More," she breathed.

He silently obliged, dipping his head to lick and nibble her collarbone. Claws traced her thigh as he coaxed the hem of the old-fashioned nightgown up, all the while ravishing her mouth with his. Her thighs fell open and he shifted between them, dragging his teeth down her neck.

The fur on his legs was shorter than on his back and arms, and it scratched a little against her thighs. The hard weight of his cock was heavy on her stomach.

His movements were more gentle than she'd anticipated, but there was nothing gentle about the look in his smoldering amber eyes when he drew back to ease the gauzy garment over her head. The fabric got stuck underneath her. She tried to wriggle out of it, but his face contorted into what must have been a silent growl, and he used a retractable claw to slice it up the middle, then pushed the torn pieces aside to free her breasts. He loomed above her, his severe gaze lingering over every part of her body. She took the moment to admire him, too, and what she saw made her her whimper.

Large did not begin to describe him. She was taken aback by the size of it and suddenly wondered if she'd made the wrong decision. There was no way he would fit inside her! So much for being the tight hole he longs for. Surely there was no pleasure in seeing a small hole he had no hope of fitting into. Would she even be able to wrap her mouth around it?

Oblivious to her darkening musings, the mahr leaned down and buried his head in her breasts. He lay there, head between her boobs and cock throbbing against her torso, for so long that she wondered if he was just going to fall asleep like that. Could he fall asleep in a dream? She trailed her fingernails through the fur on his back and then gave a little tug, which seemed to get him back in motion. He leaned onto his elbows and licked her breast, starting at the crease where it squished against her torso and going all the way to her pert nipple. The look on his face was pure bliss, like he would willingly give such avid attention to her chest for hours and hours, licking her sweat and burying himself in her underboob just to be near it. The sweet sight made her heart flutter, but it also made her pussy pulse with need. She gyrated her hips against him, trying to create the friction her body required.

The lucid part of her felt her body in the bedroom. Something brushed against her bare skin underneath the towel, which had fallen open.

The mahr's fangs teased her nipple, then he moved lower, dragging his teeth and tongue down to the tightly wound bundle of her need. He wrapped his furry biceps under her thighs and gave a sharp yank until his hot breath bristled against her clit. She rocked her hips, seeking whatever he would give her, but he held her in place. He looked up at her mischievously and she moaned, the sound a primal plea that surprised her.

"More. More, please, don't stop."

Two sharp fangs sank into her inner thigh. Not hard enough to make her bleed—could she bleed in a dream?—but the sudden adrenaline sent electricity through her, bouncing between her flushed cunt and the tips of her peaked nipples like the prongs of a taser.

Wetness surged between her thighs, his tongue quick to lap it up. She moaned and writhed against his broad tongue, her body moving of its own accord. She leaned onto her elbows to watch as he sucked her clit rhythmically until another wave of liquid heat rushed to her cunt. He slurped it up like she was the tastiest bowl of soup and he wanted to savor each drop. The sight made her need to be filled by him grow exponentially. She fell back and bucked her hips, riding his face like a maniac as he drank every last drop of her weeping cunt.

His finger slid between her drenched folds. She leaned onto her elbows again and met his fervent gaze, his mouth a suction on her clit. She tilted her hips to engulf his finger and rode it until he gave her another and another. Her slick inner walls cinched against his fingers and her orgasm forced her onto her back to ride out the undulating crests of pleasure, all the while her mahr sloppily drank each drop of fluid that flowed from her cunt.

Satisfied and yet hungrier than before, she lay back and panted until her breathing returned to normal. Her cunt fluttered around nothingness as she retracted, still twitching with pleasure, and yet the ache remained. The mahr lay languidly between her thighs, his head resting on her leg. He appeared to be smelling her, which she found both sexy and endearing, and she wondered if he was done with her.

"What about you?" she asked, though what she really wanted to say was *give me that cock, even if it doesn't fit, give it to me anyway*.

His smile was tight-lipped and forlorn as he gave a slight shake of his head. He slipped from her legs to hover over her. He beckoned her and she readily accepted his hand, casting aside the lingering need to be filled.

Disappointed but sated, Addison didn't dare mention his promise had only been for one dream when he didn't get rid of the pleasant dream like he'd threatened. The nightmares didn't return. Instead, they traveled the world, taking on the form of many animals, from hawks soaring above to otters chasing each other in the waves.

Some of the lands they explored looked like photographs from inspirational posters, while some seemed so old they couldn't possibly still exist. It was obvious the mahr held these places with deep regard by the way he watched intently for her reactions. They soared over the ocean and she leaned down to run her fingers through the water, laughing at the spray. They passed an active volcano, the heat reaching her face even from a good distance away. They raced against the side of a great cavern filled with crystals larger than her whole body. They walked the cobbled path of an old town decorated with odd architecture, where her shoulder passed through a resident with pointed ears.

It was all so surreal, Addison almost forgot it was a dream. These places had to be real—it was the only explanation. He was sharing intimate details of the places he'd witnessed while traveling the world distributing nightmares.

Spongy moss kissed her toes as they touched down in a valley nestled between two great mountains. Waterfalls beaded the mountainside and twilight's light cast a pink hue to the quaint field, where goats grazed and little sprouts of some unknown plant lined the ground. He approached a short wooden fence that enclosed a little cottage.

"Is this place special to you?"

The rueful look in his eye as he watched the thatch-roofed home was answer enough.

The door opened with a squeak. A handsome man emerged with shearing tools in hand and greeted the woolly sheep with a series of affectionate murmurs. The beautiful elf from her dreams.

He wore trousers, boots, and a loose-fitting tunic, his pale hair pulled back with a ribbon, a stylish bun that showed off his point-tipped ears. His chiseled cheekbones and hooked nose were unmistakably that of the mahr's, but when he smiled at the woman following him out the door, the smile was warm and friendly; nothing like the wolfish, animalistic grin she'd come to crave.

The woman was much older than him. She wore a scarf over her shoulders and patted his cheek affectionately, saying something in a language Addison didn't understand.

Her heart ached when she turned to see the mahr's pinched frown. He stared at the scene for a moment longer before waving his hand, transforming the view back to that of the blooming field of lavender he'd ravished her in.

He brushed his fingers against her cheek. Addison held it there and nuzzled his palm, peppering kisses to his wrist.

"Thank you for sharing that with me," she whispered. "I'm sure it was painful."

His eyes, bright and keen, locked on hers. The breath left her lungs for a moment, fleeing the severity of his stare, which held more raw emotion than she'd honestly thought a demon capable of. He was nothing like she'd assumed a *demon* would be. She wanted to know all of him, from his innermost feelings to the more primal ones that drove him to her chest each night. For a demonic spirit, he was so gentle and caring, so eager to please her. Could their connection be more than just physical? She didn't even know his name.

Lost in thought, she startled when the mahr leaned his forehead against hers and kissed her slowly, tenderly, his two fanged teeth grazing her bottom lip. She purred and deepened the kiss, flattening her hands against his back and burrowing her fingers into his fur coat.

"Let me pleasure you," she murmured as she nuzzled his cheek. "Please. You've done so much for me."

It was true. Aside from the earth-shattering orgasm, the demon had given her a dream unlike any other. It was so beautiful, crisp, and real that she wondered if she'd ever dream of anything else again. Every night, she would long to be back here, soaring over incredible beauty and laughing at the spray of the ocean. He was so open and vulnerable when he truly didn't have to be. He *wanted* to show her his past and share his little piece of the world. It was obvious he loved to travel, but she also saw a wound in his heart that she found herself deeply longing to fill.

A lascivious grin graced his lips, but still he shook his head. He pulled her onto his lap and held her like a bundle in his arms as the sweet dream unfolded all around her. She drank it all in as her attention span got shorter and shorter until she fell into a sleep so deep she surely wouldn't remember anything else once she awoke.

By the time her alarm went off, Addison had no idea what they'd been doing for the remaining hours. "Good morning." His deep, gravelly voice coaxed her heavy eyelids open. He sat cross-legged on her chest, his shadows faintly whipping and flickering in the approximation of his bite-sized bodily form.

"Good morning," she greeted. A giddy smile teased her lips and she instinctively moved to lay her hands on his knees, but her palms were met with cool air that held only a trace of solidity, not the real-feeling body that had been in the dream. "Why can't I touch you?"

"Dreams allow me to be closer to my mortal self, but here I can only become strong enough for this." He gestured to himself and transitioned from her chest to the bed beside her. "In either form, I cannot feel things, not completely."

"That sounds lonely." It also explained why he didn't want her to even attempt to please him. She assumed it would only make him feel worse to not actually get to experience it. "Thank you. For tonight, for everything—and for sharing your memories with me."

"I'd forgotten their faces. I'm surprised I was able to unearth them after all this time," he whispered. His nebulous eyes took on a faraway glaze that made Addison's heart ache for him, but he shook his head and it quickly disappeared. "You're welcome, dreamer. I hope it was satisfactory."

He suddenly stood and hovered beside her bed, his shadows writhing and gaze drifting to the ceiling. The sight of him feeling awkward was odd. She narrowed her eyes and waited for an explanation.

"I will need to feed on some sleepers in order to…" He cleared his throat and glanced at the ceiling once more before addressing her again. This time, his voice held his typical timbre, though his veneer of aloofness didn't fool her anymore. "I would like to return tonight."

"Yes," she agreed readily, heart fluttering in her chest. "I would like that."

Chapter 14
Traeyr

His dreamer knew not what she did to him.

When she'd inquired on his pleasure the first time, right after he selfishly drank his fill of her savory liquids, Traeyr wanted her so badly he could have lost control and accidentally crushed her in the waking realm. It was thoroughly painful to deny himself, but he wouldn't dare risk hurting her. In the mortal realm, his body grew so full of power that he was nearly completely material. He'd ridden her chest feverishly, fueled by her desire and the intoxicating scent of her liquid heat, all for him. It was with great reluctance that he was able to force his retreat, watching her face soften in both realms as she was overcome by her orgasm. He longed to fill her mouth as she formed the words, voicing her concern for his own satisfaction.

After showing her his favorite places from all his travels, he hadn't consciously made the decision to share his most painful moment. The last time he saw his mother. Something compelled him to open what was left of his heart with the human. Addison's empathy and compassion were too much. He'd cowardly whisked them away, back to the field of her pleasure to allow sleep to overtake her. He watched her dream peacefully, the soft lines of her face more captivating than any of the memories he had stored away. The weight of her in his arms, the trust she placed in him, it all combined to create the perfect avalanche, crashing down the mountains built around his lost soul.

Tonight he would not have such willpower.

Daylight made sleepers scarce, but Traeyr worked with unwavering resolve. His hunt for victims would not be discouraged. Towers of glass soared high into the sky, housing millions of cubicles with slumped sleepers. The next town over was populated by hundreds of square apartments. In the surrounding rural area that stretched farther and farther from Addison's keyhole lay fields of innocent animals who believed themselves above his dark touch.

Nothing was above him this day. He would ride her chest tonight. He would not deny her again.

He'd never come so close to giving his name freely to anyone. In his many centuries, his name had remained safely guarded. It died with his body and then perished for good when all who'd known him passed away. There was no one left alive capable of trapping him. He vowed not to let his infatuation with this dreamer be the end of his travels. He would allow the beautiful mortal to bring him to new heights and show him just how much he was capable of feeling in his insubstantial body. After he gleaned the pleasure of her tight holes, he hoped the infatuation with her saporous liquids and satiating nightmares would fade.

Power bristled through every strand of hair that coated his partially substantial form. He held his hands before him and watched the padding of his palms crease and flex as he curled and uncurled his fists. Even with this much nightmare residue, he did not have a fully engaged sense of touch. He leaned down to stroke the woolly coat of a sheep as he strode through the pen. The awareness of feeling was there, and the animal responded to his touch, but for Traeyr it was a phantasmal experience that he knew was a fraction of the real thing.

Not only would his plan tonight require a great amount of power in order to bring him the most sensation possible, it also required he keep his wit under rigid control. In having so much power stored, he put Addison at greater risk underneath him. He must remain disciplined even as he crested the waves he wished to wring from his willing dreamer. A stronger man would not risk her in that way, but he was not a man and he *could not* deny her again.

A strong, unmistakable scent of musky earth and moldy dirt snatched his awareness the moment he reached Addison's neighborhood. He followed the scent to a keyhole mere houses down.

The waning light of dusk cast long shadows along the curbside. With a flick of power, Traeyr banished the shadows to locate the putrid night hag under what light remained of the sun. The wraith hissed and dug her claws deeper into the siding of a yellow-painted home. Her head swiveled backward in a creaking motion before she scuttled over the roof on all fours and dove into an open window.

Traeyr snarled, then howled, asserting his dominance to all night creatures in the vicinity. There would be no feasting anywhere near his dreamer's scent. Her dreams were his alone.

He no longer contained as much power as he'd set out to gain before their meeting tonight, but he would not leave Addison's room vulnerable. To save what he had managed to gather, he shrank to his butterfly form, then he slipped through her keyhole. The undulating sensation of the crevice was a tease for what was to come.

When the sound of the lock mechanism clicking into place announced his dreamer's arrival, he let go of his power and greeted her with a sly grin.

"Well, hello there," she purred. She tossed a ring of keys onto the desk haphazardly, knocking over the wooden structure there. "Oh, sorry, Stevie."

Charmed by her strangeness, Traeyr felt movement inside his black heart. It felt akin to the giddiness one found within a child's untainted dreams, eager to learn and play. This peculiar feeling was something to examine later, but now, he just wanted to learn more about his human and play with their odd connection.

"I gotta say, it's nice coming home to someone." She fixed the wooden man and then busied herself around the room.

I could be here every night. The thought rose unbidden and he scowled at its unwelcome disturbance. *This is a one-night thing.* Two, technically, if he were to include the night before. It was all merely a ploy to get her out of his system. Not a surrender to entrapment.

Then he read the unspoken words within her statement and realized it wasn't about him at all.

"You miss your human lover."

"Justin? No." Addison's face scrunched. She made a little retching noise. "He didn't get so happy to see me. He sure as hell didn't look at me like that."

She gestured to Traeyr's face, her own tinting a complementary shade of pink. "What do I look like?"

The pink of her cheeks enhanced and she gestured helplessly. "Like you want to eat me or something."

"I plan to do more than eat you."

He relished the way her eyes widened, her mouth opening. His eyes lingered on her parted lips, his dirty thoughts turning to absolute filth.

"Stay here. I have to shower real quick," she said with a playfully demanding tone.

She knew he could follow. He was aware that she'd seen him follow last night, knew that he'd witnessed her little tease. But this time he would obey, knowing that what she wanted was for him to follow.

She would not always get what she wanted.

"Where shall we travel tonight?" he asked when she returned.

To his delight, she twisted a flimsy towel around her chest and jumped into bed. He followed and drifted above her, careful to only allow enough of his body to be outlined for her to be at ease, to not feel like she was speaking to a disembodied ghost, and no more. His shadows whipped and clawed at the seams of his hold, but he remained steadfast as he straddled her torso and refrained from burdening her with all of his weight. Her hands immediately went to his thighs and traced them up and down with the tips of her fingers.

"You're more…touchable than you were this morning," she observed as her faintly ticklish tracing elicited a shiver through his restrained shadows. He closed his eyes at the sensation, tightening his hold before looking back at her face to witness the perfect rounding of her lips.

I cannot give in yet. There was still a whole night ahead of him.

"I ate my fill so I would be better equipped for my plans tonight."

The smile he gave her this time was dark and promising. A surge of heat between her legs responded to his pledge and he dragged in a deep inhalation of her scent.

"In that case, I don't care where we go."

"Close your eyes."

He sent a trace of shadow over her eyelids to tease them closed. With a rush of power, he drew her below consciousness and laid her down on a raised mound of the softest pincushion moss, its velvety texture conducive to the pleasure he wished to bring her.

She laced her fingers into his and played a lazy dance with their hands. Her bottom lip slipped under her teeth and she lay back, pulling him down to drape over her. He traced the lines of her face, trailing down her slight neck and farther, over the rise of her breast and the bow of her waist, the soft skin of her stomach, then back up to her jaw. The fierce impulses that ruled his lust-filled mind paused at the faint touch, something softer stirring inside him. Something about these subdued motions felt more permanent.

Addison slipped the thin straps of the traditional elven nightgown from her shoulders, slipped her arms free, and glided the fabric over her taut nipples. She must have discerned his obsession with her lusciously ample chest—not that he'd tried to hide it—and she used it to taunt him.

She took his hand and placed it on her plump breast. He teased her nipple, rolling it between his thumb and forefinger, watching as it grew longer and tighter under his succor. She moaned in encouragement and he bowed his head to lick her other nipple, sucking it into his mouth until his fangs caressed the skin surrounding her burgundy areola.

The sounds she made punctured his control, but even if he still wanted to say no, Addison didn't seem to care. She raised one knee and splayed out the other, her eyes on him as she dipped her hand into the slickness of her glistening cunt.

Desire clouded his focus. His dark instincts wrestled for control. He wanted to pull her over the precipice and steal every drop of liquid from her leaking cunt. Wanted to feel her juices drip down his chin as he drowned himself in them, wanted to fill every tight hole in his little dreamer until she bulged and burst beneath him. In the bedroom, he sent tendrils of shadow over her sleeping body, teasing her with light touches and pinches. His cool touch made her hips buck, which in turn made him rock his own, driving his desire through her valley.

She kept her eyes trained on his as she tested his reserve. Her lips formed the perfect O and he reached his fingers to her mouth. She sucked them seductively, sending another wave of rebellion through his fraught control. He hooked his fingers in her mouth and leaned down to lick the inside of her lips, exploring the inside of her cheeks with his tongue. Retreating, he tilted his head to the side and used his most covetous expression to tell her exactly where he wanted to be.

Her gaze intensified. She nodded eagerly, sucking his fingers back into her mouth.

Straddling her in the waking world and in the dream, he slid his cock between her breasts. She held them together and watched his face. Even in his half-mortal body that didn't truly have flesh, it felt exquisite to ride her chest the way he'd imagined a thousand times. This was the closest he could recall to feeling alive in all his memory. He placed his hands on either side of her head and slowly glided his cock up her valley and over her eager tongue.

The shadows obeyed his call and he sent them over her legs. He splayed her thighs wide and slid open her damp folds to reveal the hidden nub that held her pleasure. He wanted her to feel the way he felt, to show her how grateful he was for her willingness to act out his deepest desires.

She moaned against his cock and he seized the opportunity. He rose on his knees and slid into her mouth, her perfect lips straining to encase him. Meanwhile, he sent his shadows in search of her openings. Without entering yet, he teased them both by coating her with her own slickness, from her swollen, needy clit to her puckered ass. As gentle as he could muster, he repeatedly slammed his cock to the back of her mouth, relishing the sound of her gags until being so near to the heat of her tight holes while his cock was in her mouth became too much.

Oh, goddess! Her petite human cunt was so small, so tight his shadows strained to fit!

The ridges of her slippery walls squeezed his shadows, almost causing him to lose grip on his power. Her cunt leaked around his shadow tendril. He had to pause to regain composure. Addison met his struggling gaze and the side of her mouth curved upward around his throbbing length. She raised her neck and he quickly reached to steady her. She kept her eyes intent upon his as she suctioned her mouth around the bulb of his head, her cheeks concaved as she sucked hard, determined, unflinching, soft hands pumping and caressing his shaft.

Absently, he remembered to imbibe the nightmares that pushed the boundaries of her sleeping mind, attempting to creep in unnoticed by his protective shield. The bedroom was filled with the aromatic scent of her desire. It invigorated him more than when he ate her dreams, which surprised and thrilled him.

The small piece of his cognizance holding him back from crushing her became a fragile shell threatening to burst, but he could not stop now that he'd allowed himself this far.

Chapter 15
Addison

Addison had never been so turned on by giving a blow job in her life. The fact that he was clearly captivated by anything involving her chest and her mouth made it all the sexier to watch him extract exactly what he needed from her. His fetish could be watching her smash cupcakes on her face or something she found equally confusing and she would still be turned on just to know he was taking what he desired from her body, using her. It felt good, so good, to know she was finally giving him the same happiness he'd given her.

He retreated from her mouth and shifted lower. He took hold of her knees and slipped them over his thighs, then guided her over him until she sat above his lap with his lengthy cock between them and her slickness rubbing against the bottom of his shaft. He ravished her neck, collarbone, and breasts with his fangs and his tongue. She took the opportunity to stroke the ridges of his horns, which sent a tremble through his shoulders.

She giggled, pleased to have found a new erogenous spot on his body.

"Does that feel good?"

His lips curled in a silent growl. He bit down on a meaty bite of her breast in answer. She gasped in surprise and kept teasing his horns, then reached down with one hand to stroke him, pressing the wide tip of his cock between her breasts until it sank into her cleavage. For the second time since meeting him, she felt immensely grateful for her large breasts, which had been a source of insecurity ever since they'd played a major role in an instance of her past when she'd matured faster than other girls her age. This man—demon—was enthralled by her chest, and whether the size of her breasts played into his obsession or not, it certainly aided her in her quest to send him over the edge.

She stroked from his base, which was a few fingers' length below her belly button, to just under his tip where it disappeared in her cleavage, and moaned against his mouth. She drove her hips over him repeatedly, rocking against his solid sack and coating his fist-sized balls with her juices.

"More," she moaned.

She could feel him in her bedroom. She felt the pressure of him riding her chest the same way he'd done in her dream moments ago, and it turned her on to know he was still fucking her breasts the way he liked. It thrilled her that he was getting off in so many more ways than she could imagine. What must that be like, to be pleasured in two realms at once? The thought made her clit pulse with need, begging for his touch.

She wasn't sure how to fit them together, but she was getting desperate to feel his cock deep inside of her guts. She rose onto her knees and took hold of his thick length, deciding she would wait no longer, but before she could work out the schematics, he gruffly laid her back down onto the velvety-soft bed of moss.

He lined up his cock with her entrance and pressed forward agonizingly slow. It didn't hurt to be stretched by him, but she figured that was thanks to this being a dream and not reality. In reality, she knew it would be painful to receive a cock of his length and girth. Instead, it felt like a steady pressure as he slid inside of her, pausing every few moments to stay in control.

She tried to move against him, to let him know it was okay, that she wanted his huge cock to fill every crevice inside her; but her body became rigid. In the bedroom, she could feel the cold weight of his shadows restraining her, and even in the dream she was unable to fight against his strong hold. Struggling against him only strengthened his bonds. All she could do was whimper her disapproval.

"Fill me, please. I want you so bad."

Her mahr met her pleading gaze and gave her a primal grin, the carnal look in his eyes belying how badly he wanted to do exactly that. Still, he returned to his excruciating work, entering her inch by inch, her body deemed useless against his powerful hold. Her inner walls slowly accustomed to his width, her body yielding to him with every shallow thrust.

When he was finally sheathed inside her, the pressure of his thick cock sent waves of pleasure through her core. Her body pulsed to the rhythm of his throbbing muscle where it reached all the way to her guts and slowly massaged the inside of her walls with his slow pace. It felt so good, she was sure she would have passed out if not already in a dream.

His magic never released its grip on her limbs, his face a rictus of pleasure and control. She longed to rip that control from him, to render him as reckless and carefree as she felt in this moment, but it was clear that something beyond her knowledge forced him to refrain.

As he pumped inside of her, his bondage loosened enough for her to raise her hands and pet his shoulders, mewling and crying out in ecstasy. Through the blinding waves of pleasure, she remembered his weakness and traced the ridges of his horns, which made him rut into her sopping wet cunt harder.

Yes, yes, lose control for me. She lifted both hands to his horns, stroking and tracing them and eventually grabbing them to keep her wits as his strokes became more and more wild, his release climbing to the same tempo as the quivering of her cunt.

His head reared back. His jaw opened in a silent roar she felt reverberate through their connected bodies. He stilled, and she grinded her hips against him, using her inner walls to wring every last drop from him until her own orgasm forced her body still and she twitched with the torrent of come streaming inside her, pleasure wracking through her every muscle.

Distantly, she felt the pressure on her sleeping body increase. For a moment, she felt she couldn't breathe inside their dreamlike cocoon, like the air was being blocked from her lungs. But the pressure eased as her mahr's expression grew more lucid and he leaned onto his elbows above her, his expression both worried and deeply affectionate. He dusted a hair from her forehead and nuzzled her neck, inhaling deeply.

The passionate session exhausted her even in this unconscious landscape. It seemed to exhaust him too, because he rolled them to the side and pulled her head against his chest. He took her hand and pressed her knuckles to his lips, playfully biting her thumb with a fanged tooth, then peppering the top of her head with more sweet kisses.

They lay that way for what felt like ages, snuggled inside of a dream.

Chapter 16
Addison

Addison woke to find the mahr perched cross-legged on her chest, one hand propping up his head, the other stroking her cheek. When her eyes opened, he floated to the side and gave her a warm smile that only held an ounce of its usual swagger.

"Good morning." His voice was deliciously deep. The heat in his black eyes sent fireworks through her belly.

"It's good to hear your voice."

Here he was immaterial, though at least he wore his familiar form and not the butterfly. Her gaze drifted to the flickering tips of his horns, memories of their shared dream filling her with warmth. She extended her hand but caught herself, knowing it would not be the same as merely moments ago, but he didn't miss her impulse to reach for him.

"Your dream sap will wear off and then I'll have only shadow."

"Sap?" She giggled at his word choice.

"How long do you have?"

"I don't know. I've never…I've never been so well-nourished before." He smirked at some inside joke she didn't fully understand, though she knew it had something to do with the sex. The answer to her earlier question made something inside her tummy flip in validation. Then it was true that what they shared was special compared to how he felt about all of his victims.

"I've never been so full before, either," she enunciated with a wiggle of her brows. "Is that a challenge, dreamer?" he asked darkly. "Because I happen to know you can be filled much more."

His suggestive tone sent heat trickling to her cunt. A tendril of shadow rose from his body to tickle the side of her mouth, while another pressed against her still-slick folds, and yet another pressed against her ass.

"Oh!" Her eyes widened with realization. "Oh, god, yes!"

His hearty laughter at her eagerness made her feel a little silly but no less starved for the sensation. She playfully swatted his chest, but he brushed his cold lips against her forehead. Her phone blared the alarm and buzzed violently against the nightstand. Addison groaned.

"Ugh, I have to work today."

The thought of the loud, stinky fish market made all the heat dissipate from her post-sex euphoria. A streak of inspiration had blossomed from the incredible night of unperturbed sleep and the best sex of her life—despite it being in a dream—that she just wanted to stay home and mess around with all the unfinished projects she'd collected since college.

Maybe Leah would cover me. Her shift wasn't for another few hours. It couldn't hurt to ask.

"Would you hang out with me today?" she asked her demon. "I shall stay as long as possible." "Oh." She quirked her brow and protruded her lip in a mock pout. "You have chests to ride on the other side of the world?"

"It took a great deal of power not to crush you." He watched her process the disturbing tidbit of information. It did put his intense control under perspective. "I'll need to replenish for what I have in store tonight."

She grinned. The further affirmation that their connection was more than that of a demon riding its victim filled her with joy. She tried to tame her excitement before answering too eagerly.

"That sounds lovely."

His posture loosened and he nodded. "Good. Then yes, I shall remain with you until I require nourishment."

"Can't you just make me nap?"

"I cannot force sleep while the sun shines."

That made sense, however disappointing it was.

Her phone buzzed.

"Leah agreed to work for me! Do you wanna see the artwork I'm doing for my friend?"

She stood from the bed. A little flicker of shadow pinched her nipple with its cool touch, making her yelp.

She'd forgotten she was naked for their entire conversation. Slipping into a T-shirt, she plopped into the computer chair. The mahr followed and peered over her shoulder.

"I've been working on it for a while now. Too long, really. It's what I love, though. I wish I could quit this stupid job and make art full time." She pulled up the design and watched as he scrutinized it, trying to gauge his thoughts from the shadows forming his features.

"You are exceptionally talented. I'm certain you would do well following your dream."

Addison smirked at his curt assessment and started working on it while he watched over her shoulder.

"So, is it possible to…you know…break your curse?" She peered at him askance and watched the wall of stoicism fall into place. "I mean, we don't have to talk about it."

"No. The man who did this to me is long dead." He flitted gracefully from one side of her chair to the other, remaining condensed enough that he only towered a foot above her and not several. She could tell there was more to the story, but she didn't press the issue. Surely she would be grumpy, too, if someone had stripped her mortality.

"Addison, do you realize your nightmares are summoning dark creatures determined to possess you? I believe we should remedy this instead of entertaining lost causes such as my soul."

Addison blanched. "*What?* Way to change the subject. Were you going to tell me about this?"

"Of course."

She scoffed and stood, gesturing for him to elaborate.

"Do you recall the hag?"

"The zombie lady with the nasty hair? Yes." Unfortunately. She wished she could forget the feel of those long, jagged, dirty fingernails against her skin and the high-pitched laughter that seemed to invade her dream. "I saw you that night, standing on top of me."

"Yes. I asserted my dominance but have since spotted another of her kind encroaching upon my territory." Addison narrowed her eyes. "Territory? What, my bedroom?"

"Yes." His form bristled outward until he grew in size to loom over her, but his intense gaze held heat and fierce protectiveness. He bared his teeth. "Your nightmares are mine, Addison. I refuse to share them with another demon or wraith, no matter how powerful. You are mine."

The intensity in the way he claimed her, coupled with the terrifying form his shadows took as they whipped around him, should have scared her. Seeing him like this, his fathomless eyes glowing a deep yellow-orange like the heat of a fire, every shadow in the room rushing to join his fray, reminded her that he was a demon.

A demon she'd allowed to ride her and almost *crush her to death* just for the sensation of his cock buried deep into her dreaming body.

But she wasn't afraid. Not even a little.

"You've been protecting me before I even knew you were real. Haven't you?"

He didn't shrink back from her accusation. On the contrary, he growled like a beast in the wild, his gaze taking on an even more terrifying glow.

"I've known since the first night I detected your scent, well before you caught me feasting on your tears. Even as I hid the truth from myself, I knew I could not allow you to fall into the possession of another. I refuse to lose you, dear dreamer. Including to the depths of your own nightmares."

Addison closed the distance between them. She realized his show of fearsome power was a front for his concern for her, and while she couldn't touch him the same as she'd done last night, she tenderly cupped the cold air of his cheek and met his glowing yellow gaze until he softened.

"Thank you."

The fire blazing in his eyes slowly snuffed out. He nodded curtly and gestured back to her computer screen.

"Continue. As you work, tell me about the human named Addison."

She snorted. "All right, but it's pretty boring."

"A boring life does not incur such horrors that draw wraiths from the underworld."

"Fair enough."

She knew he referred to the traumas that led to her twisted dreams, but she launched into the more lighthearted details all the same, like how she'd grown up on the beach. She mentioned being bullied in school and the frenemies who sometimes appeared in her nightmares as a remnant of her inner child's pain, and about college and how she'd wound up working at a fish counter instead of utilizing her design skills because of Justin.

"The man who broke into your home," he interrupted with a sneer.

"Yeah. My ex. Looking back, I think I was in love with the idea of being needed by someone more than I loved Justin himself." She shrugged. "We were supposed to live here together, but he said I was a needy bitch and left me with all the bills."

A growl emitted from his throat, something entirely inhuman and more violent than she'd heard from him before. The sound reminded her again that he was, in fact, a demon, and not just a gentle lover. "Good."

"*Good*?"

"Yes. I would have had to crush him in his sleep." He licked his lips. "You are *mine*."

Another thrill shot straight through her core. "Well, I hope you like a *needy* lover."

"You don't know needy."

What the hell does that mean? Before she could ask, his shadows caressed her skin and she closed her eyes to the cool sensation.

"And what of the night terrors? There must be something in your history. Perhaps if you share it with me, I can be of assistance in healing what festers within your subconscious. It is imperative we get your dreams under control, for there are creatures even I would be incapable of protecting you from."

Flashbacks of hot brandy-soaked breath banished the happiness from his soft caress. Her mother's contorted face in the doorway, smelling of the same brandy that licked Addison's neck.

She hesitated. She stared down at her lap, unwilling to watch his reaction as she spilled her dirtiest laundry.

"When I was fifteen, my mom's boyfriend of the month kept hitting on me. He would make sure to be in the spaces he knew I occupied." Addison absently rubbed the back of her neck, where the feeling of warm, wet breath suddenly lingered. She laid her hands palm up against her knees and took a steadying breath. "He took me to the mall and bought me stuff. I thought it was cool, and my mom liked that we were getting close even though she barely knew him."

The mahr stayed quiet, his comforting touch never wavering from its semi-solid place behind her. The computer timed out and she glanced up to see his shadows dancing in the black screen.

"Anyway. When he finally made his move, I was too scared to run. My mom found us like that and said I seduced him. She eventually apologized, but by that time it had been years of internalizing the awful things she said to me that night."

Addison ended on a shrug and glanced over her shoulder without looking high enough to meet his gaze. "It was so long ago. It's no big deal."

"Addison."

At the iron in his voice, she summoned the courage to meet his eyes, which shone with the intensity of a thousand sunsets. His fangs were out and his gentle but firm tone was resolute.

"You were just a child."

She rolled her eyes. "Humans call fifteen a *young adult*. We're expected to be thinking about what career we want. Hell, if we commit a crime at fifteen, we could be tried as an adult in some cases. Maybe for elves it's different—"

"Human or elf, the first fifteen years are developmental. You. Were. Only. A. Child. You could not have been expected to navigate a situation like that. You certainly could not be held accountable."

The ferocity in his voice was nothing like the degrading tone of her mother. It was different than the hunger he usually showed her. This was something new, something that sent chills through her body. Tears pricked her eyes and she dropped her head.

The mahr's cool touch never left her, but he maneuvered to her side and coaxed her chin to face him. His shadows lowered until they were eye level. The compassion in his dark features astounded her.

"Let go of that shame. It is not necessary." He leaned forward and licked a tear before it made its descent. "You are safe. Set that little girl free. She did the best she could. She kept you alive. Now let her go."

His words shattered her. They didn't sound much different than the things Dr. Ellis drilled into her, but somehow they were an entirely new revelation coming from him. Dr. Ellis had to say those things, no matter how true. But this demon, this creature of the dark who'd seen inside her head and watched her nightmares unfold, he had no reason to absolve her. No reason to remain by her side after witnessing the darkest corner of the ruins remaining of her memory palace. Yet here he was, for the second morning in a row, staying with her after safeguarding her dreams all night long.

The dam broke. All the tears she'd held inside, smothered under the sound of blaring music or hidden by withholding sleep from her body, flooded her cheeks and made her shake. The mahr never broke their contact, until finally she was able to breathe again, her lungs becoming full as her mind was cleared, a weight of guilt lifted from where it had taken permanent hold on her psyche.

The afternoon's light pierced through the blinds as she worked on the book cover. As time passed, the mahr's shadowy edges slowly became less and less defined. She knew he would have to leave soon when he faded into the small butterfly and perched on her hand, his wings flickering like the wick of a candle.

"Tonight, wait until I am in your room. Then plug all the holes in your home," he said, his soft voice coming from the little insect. "I'll help you locate them. Then lie down, and when you feel me on your chest, say Traeyr."

"What's Traeyr?"

"My name."

The day passed slowly. A warm haze encompassed Addison's unburdened mind. She almost felt lightheaded with all the freed-up space in her head, though she knew that would pass and that healing was not a one-and-done deal. Still, for once it felt like everything was going to work out. Even missing a day of work wasn't upsetting her inner peace.

Taking a break from the cover, she checked her email to see a notification of a job listing from The Idea Initiative, a reputable design agency renowned for their work from web design to games, illustrations, and more. *What the hell. Why not?* She submitted her portfolio and even took the time to write an eloquent cover letter.

She tapped her finger on the golden cap of the small jar holding her wishes. It had been a while since she'd put anything new inside it, but the jar was a visual reminder that she was working toward something. She unscrewed it and poured the folded pieces of paper onto her desk.

All the scraps said something that could be bought, like a house on the beach, a road trip vehicle, a nicer laptop. She plucked a notebook from the box at her feet and considered what she would write if she were being truly honest with herself.

Peaceful sleep.
Self-acceptance.
To feel safe.
A place to belong. A loving home.
Someone who thinks of me as their home.

Thanks to Traeyr, she was feeling closer to the first two. As for a loving home, she knew she would find that living with Marissa. But what would it be like to find a home in someone's arms? Someone who felt the same safe, loving care in her caress? She'd spent so long locked in a relationship just because she was desperate to be needed. Despite that Dr. Ellis had helped debunk her desire to be useful by tracing it back to her childhood and growing up with an alcoholic caregiver, she still wanted to find someone who would call her embrace their home. To love and be loved, and all that.

A few minutes after completing Marissa's witchy cover and sending the attachment, her phone lit up with Nasty Nathan's ringtone.

"Hello?"

"Get your ass in here now!"

"Leah's covering for me—"

"Leah's fired, and you're next if you don't get here in the next twenty minutes! I swear to god!" The line clicked.

Addison's heart sank. She would have to muddle her way through work and wouldn't get home until late. Fridays were their busiest nights. Everyone had to work an extra hour, and if she got held up, it could be well past nine o'clock before she got home.

Don't give up on me, Traeyr.

Chapter 17
Traeyr

The day-sleepers were lucky Traeyr's mind was elsewhere, his heart captured by his human, his thoughts held captive by the memory of her. Her scent, her sweet, sweet sap, her bright inner light. There was nothing he didn't love about the woman Addison. He perused the neighborhood and adjoining rural areas, reminiscing on their time together and imbibing nightmares. He would be content to laze about in her room all day, to listen as she unburdened herself, to watch the light of her passion exude from her gaze as she worked on her artwork. But to do so required strength. There were other things he'd love to do with—and to—his human, but all of it required sustenance.

Giving her his name was a risk. There were moments through the day that a dark part of his conscience nagged him. For centuries and centuries, he'd had one rule above all: he would not be bound by a human.

But Addison wasn't any human and though she had his name, she did not know the binding ritual that was capable of trapping him in her bedroom for life. Even if she did, she was nothing like the greedy farmer and his ugly wife, who only trapped him because they wanted to abuse him.

Would it be so bad to be trapped in her chambers?

To live bound to her bedroom until death stole her away would be an honor. A privilege. To hear of her triumphs and watch her spirit grow, free from the bonds of childhood shame. To be by her side each night while her passionate heart followed its dreams, each night revisiting his treasured landscapes hand in hand. To drink from her cunt as it overflowed for him, to feel her flesh on his, no more ghostly sensations but the real thing, every night.

Traeyr smirked. He sounded like a mortal with his pithy dreams. There was to be no binding, for how could he possibly entertain forfeiting his travels for one mere dreamer? No, he would not. But he would spend their next night together with his own flesh body. Although not the one he was born with, it would serve him the highest pleasure tonight.

Another sleeper's dreams invaded his musings and he followed them to the house beside his mortal's. After consuming the wayward nightmare, he visited her bedroom window to steal a peek at the woman who'd stolen his common sense. Expecting to find her at the writing desk, the empty bedroom surprised him. The entire house was void of movement.

Where is she? He'd been there when she'd canceled her commitments, too dazed from their fucking focus on a day of trivial work. His mind immediately ruminated on the chance that she left in search of deeper knowledge of his kind to trap him against his will. As hard as he tried to banish the thought, it burrowed into his consciousness and planted seeds of growing doubt.

Have I misjudged the human? Did her seductive voice and illustrious curves cloud his judgment?

She owned his name now, for better or worse. There was always the chance he was being preposterous.

Perhaps she's in trouble. This notion was somehow even more unsettling. He found himself rushing through the keyhole of her front door, the exhilarating feeling nothing compared to his worry.

There was no sign of a struggle. All her belongings were in the same places as before as far as he could tell, though he had been captivated by her and could have overlooked some things. He alternated between his two forms as he paced the room, his heart torn between fear for himself and fear for his dreamer. Though he found himself admitting that if it were between the two options, he hoped she planned to trap him and was unharmed.

Ages later, after night had fallen and sleepers nearby beckoned him to feed on their dreams, the front door slammed open against the wall. Addison rushed in, nearly tripping on a box in the walkway. He stayed floating stalk-still in his smallest form, waiting for an explanation. She sniffled and blubbered when she saw him in her room.

Something happened. His mind thundered, wondering if it was guilt or sorrow that flooded her cheeks.

"I'm so sorry. I got called in to work. And then—and then—" She broke into something similar to laughter, the strange sound conflicting with her obvious pain.

And just like that, he saw the error in his thinking. How could he have possibly considered she'd turned on him?

His waning form flitted around her. His worry had burned through his power reserves. He lacked the necessary power to wield the shadows enough to comfort her. He eagerly drank from her leaking eyes for a jolt of power.

"And then I got fired! Fuck Nathan!" She threw her hands up, the strangled half-laughter, half-weeping sound still choking its way from her throat. The wild look in her eyes was akin to a ferocious buffalo trapped under his touch after thinking itself too good for the demon's feast. She dropped to the bed and hung her head in her dainty hands. "How will I pay for this stupid house now?"

Traeyr fluttered around her aggressively. If she did as he'd instructed, he would be better equipped to comfort her.

"I'm not in the mood, Traeyr. I don't think I can."

Annoyed at his lack of power over the situation, he lapped more of her sorrowful nectar and used the burst of power to conjure his voice. "Do as I instructed so I may console you."

Shoulders hunched, she peered at him through clumped eyelashes and nodded. She hunted through some boxes in the walkway and returned with a roll of blue tape, then followed him around the room as he showed her all the spots he could escape from. Once they were all sealed, she slid under the covers and closed her eyes. He perched on her chest and braced for the inevitable rush of ancient magic that was to come.

"Traeyr."

His name upon her lips was like a blessing even as it sent a cursed amount of pain reaming through his every fiber. He gasped for air, the need to breathe a novelty he'd not experienced in centuries. A shiver ran through Traeyr's bones, the sudden sensations overwhelming. The ancient power contorted him, rebuilt him, fleshed him out until he was fully physical. His dreamer watched the transformation with wide eyes and parted lips, lips he hoped to kiss until they were sore to ease the sadness still coating her cheeks.

Chapter 18
Addison

Shadows peeled away as flesh coated bone. His transformation lifted him from the bed, all of this taking place before Addison's wide eyes.

His body was similar to what had appeared in her dream with a few minor differences. Most of his body was coated with shiny black fur. Horns twisted above his head, and fanged teeth protruded from his grin. There was a humanoid structure underneath all the fur and his softly padded abdomen, but everything was elongated, exaggerated. He was so tall that his horns almost touched the ceiling. His hands and feet were proportionally large, but so was his enormous cock, which bulged uncovered and taunted her against his leg in its half-erect state. Just like his body, it looked much bigger and much less human than the one from her dream. Its bulbous head peeked from its covering of skin and fat veins raced down its thick shaft to the corpulent sack between his legs.

His whole being was indisputably not human, not even as human-esque as it had been in the dream. Was that his doing or the work of her own subconscious?

Either way, seeing him in a physical, touchable, lickable body did wonders to help forget her troubles. Losing that dead-end job could be a sign of something better, if only that better thing happened quickly and in a timely manner.

She pushed the stray worries away and focused on the beast in front of her.

"Traeyr," she reached for him.

"Let me hold you." More of a command than a statement, his voice made her heart flutter. His cock flexed every time he spoke, sending more heat through her and causing her to struggle to lift her gaze from the gigantic thing she hoped to be impaled by soon. "You are too beautiful to cry. I'll banish the demons that haunt you."

"You're the only demon I want."

Traeyr climbed onto the end of the bed, stalking her, his muscles flexing as he sauntered to her on all fours, long cock dragging on the comforter. *Good god, how will that thing ever fit?*

He wrapped her in his arms. She wiggled free of the blanket and allowed him to maneuver her onto his lap. When he kissed her, it was deep and hungry, and a bestial growl hummed from his throat to vibrate against her core. She moaned into the kiss, her lack of financial security already mostly forgotten in his sturdy kiss and steadfast hold.

"You deserve more than some puny employment. I've seen your talent. You are destined for greater." The way he stated it so matter-of-fact made her almost believe it, too. "Forget your troubles and allow me to show you how worthy I know you to be."

She purred at the sound of that and pressed against him, his bulge growing longer and sturdier under her lap.

Her cell phone vibrated between them. She reached into her pocket to see Marissa's name on the caller ID. She answered the call while Traeyr nipped at her neck with his fangs. He seized the opportunity her little wiggle provided to bring his cock out from underneath her, situating it under her shirt, its palm-sized bulb reaching the curve of her breast where it hung over her torso. He rubbed it in the fold there, a little bead of liquid joining the sweat of her skin.

"Hey, did you get my design?" She tried not to sound like she was currently being undressed. She tilted the phone from her ear and awkwardly allowed her shirt and bra to be pulled off her body, switching the phone to her other ear. He popped the tip of his enlarged head out from under her breast and she eyed the bead of liquid already reforming at the tip, begging for her to lick it.

"Yes, and I love it!"

"That's great! I'm so glad to hear that."

She held her voice steady even as Traeyr took her free hand and guided it around his girth, her fingers far from touching. He pressed himself against her side as they stroked him together. Arousal dripped steadily from her pussy to coat her panties and she met his eyes, carefully avoiding looking down at the glistening pearl lest she do something she wouldn't be able to hide from Marissa.

"I have even better news," Marissa said coyly. Addison tried to focus on her words. "You know the job at The Idea Initiative you responded to? I actually have a friend who works there that recognized your name. She asked to see your design, so I showed it to her."

Addison gasped, though she wasn't sure if it was from Marissa's proclamation or the bead of eager liquid Traeyr swiped her thumb over.

"Right! And guess what?"

"What?" Addison cried with a giggle.

"She loved it! You'll be hearing from them sometime this week!"

"Are you serious? Oh my god!"

"Yes! I'm so proud of you, dude! You really deserve this. Especially after that asshole Justin." Marissa's tone was bright and Addison could tell how much her friend meant the words of praise. What's better, she felt it, too.

"That's awesome. Thank you for your part in this. I really appreciate you. I'm sorry your cover took so long."

"Don't worry about it. You were going through a lot. I love you."

Addison returned her love and hung up. Before she'd even set the phone aside, she tugged off her pants and underwear, giddy with adrenaline and arousal.

"What was that?" Traeyr asked, his eyes trained on her movements as he stroked himself. In his large hand, his cock looked slightly less intimidating.

"That, sir, was very, very, very hot."

Holding her hair over her shoulders, she bent at the waist and licked the drop at the slit of his cock, relishing the saltiness it left on her lips. "And that was my friend. I got a job with a legit design company!"

Traeyr growled and grabbed her waist to pull her down, but she resisted. He scowled at her, a question in his yellow eyes.

"I have to take a shower first. I smell like fish!"

"You are incapable of smelling anything but appetizing."

He easily overpowered her. He pulled her down and flipped her onto her back. His strong, furry arms held her in place as he traveled low between her legs, one hand under the curve of her breast and the other firm on the middle of her stomach, his mouth so close to the stubble on her cunt that his warm breath tickled when he spoke.

"Didn't I say you were destined for greater?" He teased her opening with a long lick from ass to clit, sending a shiver through her that forced her hips to roll.

"I knew it." He punctuated each word with a similar lick, slowly prying her folds open to reveal the most sensitive part of her to his flat tongue. Her eyes fluttered shut as she tried to buck against him, but shadows appeared from the depths to strap her down on the bed.

"There is another important manner."

"Important?" she asked with a strangled chuckle. She raised his hand to the hard peak of her nipple and moaned when he obliged her with a roll and pinch of his fingers. "I agree. This is very important."

"Look at me."

The tone of his voice and the loss of his tongue concerned her enough to obey. She shifted onto her elbows and looked at the picturesque view of him between her legs, her gaze wandering to the elegant swirl of his horns. Forgetting his command, she reached out and traced the rigid lines of one, eliciting a canine growl and sending a plume of shadows writhing behind him. He licked the inside of her thigh and traced the spot her legs met her sex. She closed her eyes for a second, but he nipped the sensitive spot with his fangs to get her attention.

"There's something I must tell you. Then I'll leave it to you to consider."

The serious edge in his tone contradicted the way he continued to slowly lick her parted entrance, stopping just short of the nub where she wanted him the most. She tried to focus but was unsure how to respond to the conflicting messages.

"There exists a way to bind me to your sleeping chambers." His tongue dragged through her slick cunt. Her legs quivered. "I could not exist outside of it, and you would be my only source of nourishment, leaving me very reliant upon you." Another long lick, deeper this time. Her eyelids fluttered, but she caught herself before he sank his fangs into her flesh. "My very existence would be in your hands, but I would be both shadow and flesh as you see now."

He paused to flatten his wide tongue against her entrance, then dipped his head lower and did the same to the seam of her ass. A surprised yelp made her twitch against his shadow's hold, then she relaxed into the sensation with a moan. He rubbed his face against her slickness with his own satisfied groan, and she watched with a smile as he coated his face with her fluids reverently.

"We could travel anywhere I've visited within your dreams," he continued. "And you would have the power to banish me at any point, but doing so would break our connection and render me unable to visit your bedroom again."

He finished with that and buried himself in his task, overwhelming her with emotions and the strengthening need tightening within her core. She gave in momentarily, her body wracking with an upcoming orgasm, but the thought of his serious admission kept her from being able to fully let go. She buried one hand in the fur coating the back of his head and concentrated on her words.

"But you wouldn't be able to travel anymore. You love to travel," she said breathlessly. "And would my dreams be enough to sustain you?"

"I would be satisfied to share with you the beauty I have seen and experience it anew through your eyes. And"—he lifted his head to meet her eyes—"I find your dreams as sustaining as your leaking cunt."

Addison moaned and ran her hand through his fur coat up to stroke his horn with feather-soft touches. "How does it work?"

He chose that moment to suction his mouth against the throbbing nub that currently held all her self-control, along with all her strong feelings for him. She nearly came undone before he backed away and rose onto his haunches. He trailed his claw-tipped fingernails up her legs, over her thighs, and to her waist. He moved her thighs between his and stalked over her. His hard cock dragged itself against her drenched cunt, leaving a trail of slickness over her skin as he continued up her body. He straddled her and hovered on all fours, the shadows flickering around him still clearly bound to his control.

The terrifying sight of this beast blatantly hunting her should make her cower in fear like prey underneath him. His features were contorted in the bestial equivalent of pure carnal sensuality, a monster ready to devour its prey.

It was impossible to resist. She tried to lift her hips to stroke the hard length of him that hung down to drag against her stomach, tried to throw her legs around his broad hips. His adroit shadows tightened in response. She was unable to move a muscle.

"To trap a mahr, you must ensnare them while in their mortal form." He continued his slow stalk over her until his knees were on either side of her chest just under her armpits. He freed his cock and settled it on her chest, then took hold of her wrists and pulled them above her head, leaning into the motion so that his long cock drove over her mouth as it slid to cover her face. "And command he rides your chest with his flesh."

Oh, god. Addison couldn't respond because of the long, rigid cock sliding over her face, but she moaned at the way it felt to be used this way, unable to move as he repeated the motion, gliding his impossibly large appendage over her face.

But just as she thought to open her mouth and stick out her tongue, Traeyr retreated. He captured her mouth with his, exploring it with his large tongue that still tasted like her sweet desire, then went lower, until he covered her torso with his and sucked and teased her nipples.

"The choice is yours. I don't want to bind you to a needy lover, if that is such a bad thing." His throat bobbed against her breast.

She summoned all her wits and contemplated his offer while tracing the ridges of his horns. Her soft touches made him grind against her leg in a lusciously distracting way, but she forced herself to think. Her body was thrilled at the thought of having him in her bed every night, as was her heart, but she refused to agree too readily just in case there was another angle she should consider first.

"What if I were to move?"

"I would appear in your new chambers the first night."

"What if I had people over?" Could her friends handle the sight of him? She wasn't ashamed of her attraction to him, but it could make things a little awkward.

"I can cloak myself in the mind of your visitors, sort of like a dream. They will see me as I wish them to. But it is a short daydream, and I would never be able to visit the beach with you or go on human outings with your friends. And you would have to tend to me every night." He raised his head to meet hers. "You need not make your decision right now, Addison."

"Thank you. I'll think about it."

Addison nodded her appreciation and pressed a kiss to his curved horn, slipping her tongue out to lick its ridges. Then she took his hand from its perch on her stomach and brought his fingers into her mouth. "For now, I want you to fill me."

Traeyr growled a savage growl. Shadows skittered over her skin as he captured her mouth with his and moved against her, rubbing his cock against her belly as he reached below to stroke her nub. She gripped his length with both hands and shivered at the thought of him filling her.

His shadows were more material than they'd been both in her dream and in the nights prior, as though his flesh and bone body imbued them with even more substance. The first moment she felt the cool, solid shadow tease her openings, she was surprised by how similar it felt to real flesh. The tendril rubbed and teased, covering itself in her slickness and spreading the clear viscous fluid all over the inside of her thighs, all the way back into the seam of her ass. Slowly, one of Traeyr's shadows slid into her sopping cunt. It didn't grow in thickness until it slid inside her, where it began to inflate.

Addison moaned at the pressure of his shadow ballooning inside her. She inadvertently gripped his cock where it pressed between them harder, which encouraged him to inflate the shadow inside her even more, preparing her for his incredible width.

"Tell me if it's too much." His voice was hoarse.

The sliver of another shadow, this one so small it was barely a wisp, teased her ass and then slipped inside with ease without flexing her open at all. Traeyr's whole body shivered and his tongue flicked out over his fang, which he bit down on, presumably to stay in control.

"Does it feel good to you?" Addison asked as his magic settled inside of her with a dull, pulsating feeling.

"I can't explain it, but yes, fitting into your small holes gives me immense pleasure." As if to accentuate his point, all of his shadows retreated and then reentered, his whole body tensing and his muscles flexing as his head lolled.

"Better than a doorknob?"

"Infinitely better." He kissed her deeply as he began to inflate both of the pulsating shadows buried within her. "Because it is with my true mate."

To know he thought of her that way sent butterflies through her, though she supposed she should've guessed by his willingness to give up everything to be with her. The sweet fluttering feelings joined the sensual dance that had taken over every string of her muscles, her bloodstream, her core, all of it moving to a new rhythm she'd never experienced before. This new choreography was sudden and overwhelming, but it showed her the truth of what she desired more than anything else.

"Traeyr." She panted against his mouth and waited for his gaze to meet hers. "I command you to ride my chest with your flesh."

Her magnificent mahr wasted no time—or possibly he was bound by a thread of ancient magic beyond her understanding. He was on top of her instantly.

The weight of his full, flesh body was too much. Addison coughed as she struggled for air.

Chapter 19
Traeyr

The moment she spoke the words, Traeyr forcibly lurched onto her chest. Black dots blurred his vision. A vortex replaced his heart cavity. If he'd thought regaining his sense of touch had been overwhelming, it was nothing compared to the ancient binding magic that pulsed through his newly recovered veins. All he could hear was the pounding thrum of his heartbeat being pumped full of binding magic. He grimaced against the invasion, the memories of its first occurrence clouding his thoughts.

Little coughing sounds pierced the veil.

Traeyr jolted, lifting onto his haunches. He peered down at his wide-eyed dreamer, his fearless, beautiful human, so trusting and kind.

He was glad to be bound to her bedroom. Glad he'd found her, relieved that she wanted him around as much as he craved her company. No longer would he travel as a lone nomad. Even though he would physically remain in her room, they would travel together every night. He would roam the earth with his dreamer, revisiting his long-lost homeland and every century of the ever-changing landscape between then and now.

"Are you all right?" she asked. Her wide eyes were full of concern. He hadn't realized he'd been silently musing as he allowed the magic to wash through him.

"I am more than all right, darling dreamer."

Still impacted by the magic older than him, his hips lowered and rocked against his dreamer's torso. With his enormous cock buried itself in her valley, more luscious than the dip between any majestic mountains, he began to oscillate on his haunches, driving himself over her pretty face. She made the sweetest little noise and welcomed him with her tongue.

"You are sublime." He met her gaze with wide, awe-filled eyes, drinking in the sight of her between his knees. "My beautiful dreamer. Do you enjoy the way I ride your chest?"

"I do," she whimpered, the sound of her voice muffled by his smothering cock. Her petite features were even more beguiling between his knees, the dainty fingers caressing his shaft a stark, undeniable contrast of their size.

"Good. Because I will do so every night, for the rest of your mortal life."

As the magic subsided, Traeyr regained connection to his shadows. The sensation of the two tendrils already inside her combined with the gorgeous sight in front of him and her wet tongue was momentarily startling. He shivered at the overwhelming sensation and removed the shadows from her tiny human holes, earning a strangled whimper.

He couldn't slow his hips as they acted on his instinct, but he gave his dreamer the most primal grin he could muster as he regained control.

"Patience, dear dreamer."

The moment he felt contained, he plunged the shadows back inside her, just the way she wanted. He watched the expression of surprise and pleasure on her delicate features beneath his cock, drinking in the sound of her need.

He would never tire of seeing her like this, so enchanting underneath him. Just as he would never tire of filling her to her heart's content, watching her take what she needed from him the way only he could provide.

Chapter 20
Addison

Needing more, Addison pressed her hands to the smooth velvet padding that lined his muscular hips to nudge him back until she could suck his swollen tip into her mouth. Traeyr quickly tucked an extra pillow under her neck without slowing his pace. She pressed her tongue to the sensitive underside where it puckered into the tip and suctioned her mouth around him as he gingerly but repetitively hit the back of her throat. The action filled her mouth with saliva, which she allowed to sloppily spill from the seams and used to slick his shaft, using both hands to slip and slide up and down his length all the way to the heavy weight of his sack on her sternum.

The shadows filling her pussy and her ass continued to inflate, their pulsing and exploring compelling her to squeeze her cheeks tighter around his cock, her knees instinctively clenching together. She felt nearly mad with rapture, her body almost as full as it could possibly be, preparing for him to stuff her to the brim.

She had never been so blessedly, completely, utterly *full* in her entire life. Her eyes rolled back and little black dots speckled her vision, the bliss within her overwhelming. She'd watched videos of women being so luckily filled, but it had never occurred to her that she might find one man to fill all of her holes—including the one in her heart.

A warmth that had nothing and everything to do with how satisfying it felt to be full of Traeyr spread through her and she opened her eyes to gaze up at his face as he climbed in ecstasy. How perfect was it that he loved small holes and knew how to fill them all? *I am the luckiest human in the world.*

And now he was *hers*, just as she was his, and he would forever live in her home as her lover and closest confidant.

She could feel his orgasm beginning in the way he slowed his rocking hips, but he stopped and pulled away, taking Addison with him onto his lap. She fisted his fur and held fast as he supplanted her. He held her close against his chest and kissed her deeply, a promise in the way his lips moved on hers. A thick tendril of dark shadow wrapped around her waist, holding her in place above him while he rubbed himself against her with one hand, the other teasing her breast.

"Please," she panted, watching him play and wishing he were already inside her, bulging her stomach with the lump of him. He smirked at her with his signature wolfish grin and ignored her plea, opting to bury his face in her cleavage and nip at the tender skin there. An old ripple of insecurity blossomed and she tightened her fists in his fur.

"I would be most content to never see another chest." His voice was muffled, but the ardent tone was unmistakable. "I am glad you agreed to trap me."

Insecurities banished, she squirmed against the hold of his shadow tendril. In response, the shadow inside her cunt retreated in a plume of darkness, and she whimpered against the loss of the pressure. She hadn't realized just how much he'd stretched her until he began to lower her onto his massive length.

Even with his shadow's preparation, his broad head pushed the limits of her walls in the most delicious way. Pain mixed with pleasure as her body grew used to his width. Traeyr growled, the deep, bestial sound reverberating against her lungs and rattling the tenuous string tying her cunt to her heart. He entered her slowly, pausing every other moment to ravish her mouth, neck, collarbones, and breasts with his coarse tongue and sharp teeth. His panted breath was hot and frantic, yet he remained in control even as she could tell he had a fragile hold.

He was moving so slowly that she could feel his cock pulsing with the orgasm he'd denied himself in her mouth. She longed to pull him down over the precipice with her. But every time she tried to slam herself down upon him, yearning for him to round out her belly, his powerful tendrils of shade tightened their hold. She watched the thick swirling ropes of shadow wind themselves around her torso and thighs, rendering her helpless.

"Please," she begged. "I need you." "You will discover what *need* feels like soon enough, my dear dreamer."

His words, both reverent and admonishing, were punctuated with another agonizingly slow movement.

Traeyr locked his arms behind him to brace himself and watched her as he removed his shadows, using the ones around her waist to finally pull her body down the last inch, burying himself inside her.

She cried out a word that barely resembled his name and nearly forgot to look down at the swell of her stomach. She gasped when she saw it, the fat bulge of her belly proving how deep he was inside her. She traced the outline with shaky fingers, eliciting another inhuman growl from her demon.

The steady stroke of his cock rocking inside her coupled with the pulsing shadow in her ass took on a more urgent pace and she delighted in how curious he was of her insides. With each upward thrust, he paved the way for himself, her body more pliant than she'd thought possible. Her inner walls clenched around him so tightly she could feel every vein of his cock pulsing with his quickened heartbeat.

"I love the way you fill my tight holes," she panted, the pitch of her voice high and unrecognizable.

Traeyr howled in response, his arms flying to her waist and cinching them together. The velvet padding of his chest caused sweet, sweet friction against her taut nipples and she reached for his horns to provide him the same. He held her flush against him and fucked up into her with abandon. A small, cool touch of shadow pressed itself between them, teasing her sensitive clit. The sudden impact made her keen like a mewling kitten, the vibrations of an orgasm spasming from deep in her core and rippling all the way to her curling toes.

"Oh, fuck!" was the last coherent thing to slip from her lips as pleasure ripped through her, waves and waves of full-body bliss that heightened and began anew as his cock twitched inside of her. She felt the long strings of his come spurt into her steadily like the rushing stream of the waterfall they'd visited in her dream, heavy and seemingly endless. She felt the moment his seed overfilled her and some leaked out of her where her pussy clung to his length, their legs becoming a mess of both of their liquids.

The only thing that kept her from melting into a puddle herself was his strong hand behind her neck, the other wrapped around her thigh so tightly she vaguely felt his claws pierce her skin through the haze of bliss. Time became incomprehensible, everything fading to the background until all that existed was undeniable pleasure. Her orgasm could have lasted hours, she couldn't say for sure, but Traeyr was there, sharing in her euphoria the whole time.

Epilogue
Addison

Addison brought the final box into the living room.

"Thanks for your help," she told Marissa and gave her a big squeeze. "I'm so glad to be back home."

"Me too!" She held her at arm's length and gave her a *look*. "So, what time should I come back tonight to meet your man?"

Marissa was the only person who knew the full truth about Traeyr. They'd even spoken a handful of times over the phone, but Marissa was camera shy, so this would be the first time she got to see him, and he would wear his true form as opposed to the dreamlike visage of a human. Addison had originally been nervous about her reaction, but after months of watching the two closest people in her life get to know each other, she was now just excited. Marissa hadn't given her a lick of crap for being in love with a demon-slash-monster and had ooh'ed and aah'ed at their love story.

"As long as he loves you," she'd said cautiously.

To which Traeyr, who had been eavesdropping from the bed, replied, "I love my dreamer more than you are capable of comprehending."

Which of course made Addison blush and giggle like a fool and left a lasting impression on Marissa.

Presently, she smiled like a fool again and tried to keep her feet planted on the ground lest she evaporate into the air in little dewy drops of love.

"I'm not sure. He said he'll appear the first night, so just get here before it gets dark."

With a little *eek*, Marissa gave her another hug and then departed.

Addison surveyed the new house and started putting boxes in their corresponding rooms. She hadn't dared to dream in a million years that she would be able to afford a house so close to the beach, but so much had changed in the year since her breakdown to Dr. Ellis in her car outside of the ugly blue house. She had kept her follow-up appointment with Dr. Ellis, and between therapy and Traeyr's unyielding love, she'd opened up about old wounds she thought were long past. Turns out, old wounds fester even if you've spoken them out loud once or twice. It takes a lot more love and acceptance—from within and without—to truly get through traumas as dark as Addison's. All her relationships were better for it, though; Marissa hadn't realized quite how deeply she'd been bruised. Having her darkness aired out, accepted, and even validated by those she cared about felt like freedom.

With her graphic design business taking off the way it had, and by retaining her job at The Idea Initiative, she'd found the ideal place to live with her mahr. She hadn't expected to be able to afford a house like this, but this one had come on the market at exactly the right time. It featured a big, open porch that dropped right off onto the beach, the perfect spot to drag her mattress out during the days that it was nice. Who said her bedroom had to stay in one place?

Hours passed until it was finally looking like twilight outside. The doorbell rang. Marissa was the only one she expected this early, but later on, they would be joined by a few more friends coming by to see the new place and meet her fiancé.

Yes, that's right. She wanted everyone to know that what she and Traeyr had was more than some boyfriend-girlfriend situation. The two of them knew they were true mates and that they were forever bound together by magic for the rest of Addison's life, but the rest of the world couldn't possibly understand that. While she relished that sweet secret, she knew the closest they could come to being understood was to proudly profess their love to the world by way of marriage.

When she'd spoken to Traeyr about it, he'd said, "I shall bind myself to you in as many ways as you wish, my love."

Such a romantic.

"Oh my goddess, I can't wait to meet him!" Marissa squealed. She brought a charcuterie board and two bags of chips inside and marched to the kitchen island.

"Dreamer?"

Marissa nearly dropped her armful of snacks as she turned a wide-eyed swoon on Addison. "Oh my gosh. That is too cute!"

Addison's heart fluttered like the first time he'd professed his love for her. She rushed to the bedroom to meet him and stopped in her tracks.

He stood in front of the bed, bare as a babe, his giant cock swinging between his legs. As she watched, her jaw open in surprise, the enormous thing began to stand at attention. She glowered at him and snatched the blanket from the bed to toss it at his groin.

"Marissa's here!" she hissed.

"Then close your pretty mouth." He chuckled.

When the blanket was situated like a loincloth around his waist, he pulled her close and kissed her deeply. Then he promptly picked up the mattress and carried it through the doorway.

"Traeyr!" Marissa exclaimed. "It's so good to finally meet you!"

"And you," Traeyr replied. They exchanged an awkward hug and then something else—something mischievous—passed between Addison's closest friends. "I trust you are prepared?"

"I am!"

Addison peered between the two of them, her two favorite people in the world who clearly had some explaining to do. "What's going on?"

"Follow me!" Marissa sing-songed and skipped to the sliding doors that led to the porch, Traeyr following behind with the mattress.

The porch was brightly lit with fairy lights and elegant decorations, including a garland of paper butterflies that cast an enchanting shadow across the wall.

Traeyr plopped the mattress down and reached for her hands. Dazed, she accepted them and turned her narrow-eyed gaze to her best friend.

"Is someone going to explain what's happening right now?"

Marissa giggled and shared another weird look with Addison's fiancé. "Well. Traeyr called me the other day—"

"You used my *phone*? Without supervision?"

His chin tilted upward, obviously proud of himself.

"He planned all of this. When you thought I left, I ran out here and tossed it all into motion. But the credit all goes to your amazing man right here, who loves you so much it's honestly gross."

Traeyr sneered at her, but Marissa only laughed. Addison's stomach continued its rampant acrobat routine and she started to lean in for a hug, but Traeyr held her in place.

"There's more," he said and beckoned to Marissa.

"He knew you want to get married, but the logistics of that are…difficult. So I got ordained!" She gestured around the beautiful porch. "Welcome to your wedding!"

Addison's throat closed around whatever she would have said next. Tears welled up in her eyes, which Traeyr immediately lapped up. She swatted him away and slammed against him, squeezing tight.

"I love you," she blubbered.

"I love you, too, dear dreamer."

Marissa cleared her throat. "Okay, let's do this!"

After everyone had gushed over Addison's enchanting ring—which featured a jewel-encrusted alexandrite butterfly and a twisting band of rose gold—and once there was no cake nor cheese left, they said their goodbyes. Marissa was the last to leave, giving both Addison and Traeyr a tight embrace.

No one had found it odd that the mattress was in the living room since they'd literally moved in today. It was fulfilling to have her old friends back and the love of her life by her side, but now she wanted nothing more than to snuggle and make love with her demon mate.

She knew Traeyr had been thinking the same thing for the past hour by the dark looks he kept sending her way, full of heat and desire. He wasted no time in moving the mattress back out to the porch, pausing to admire the ocean, the lapping tide and the sedated depths that blended into the dark night sky.

"It's beautiful," Addison whispered as she entwined her arm in his and nuzzled against his furry bicep. "I'm so glad you're here with me."

Traeyr purred, a deep and masculine sound from within his chest. He pulled her close and caressed her cheek, sending a quiver through her body that she now associated with his touches.

"It is."

"Do you ever miss traveling?" She'd asked the question many times in the past year, but he always reassured her that she was enough.

"We travel every night, my darling dreamer. There's nothing to miss. I could be anywhere, as long as we are together."

"Then let's be in our bed."

She planted a kiss on his left nipple, eliciting another deep, reverberating purr. He walked her backward, leading her to the lush bed.

"Lay with me, wife."

She did. Just as she would every night from now on. Day and night, there was nowhere else she'd rather be than his strong, soft, loving arms, which he wrapped around her with the same reverent care that she expected of him. Cool tendrils of shadow wrapped their way around her ankles, slithering up her calves and gently parting her thighs as he rose onto his haunches. Addison reached for her husband, longing to feel the warmth of his silky, velvet-padded abdomen, to bunch fistfuls of his fur into each hand, to claim his mouth with hers; but her body didn't move more than a lurch.

She whimpered in reproach, but Traeyr's shadows whirled and whipped around her arms and legs while he loomed above, staring down with a ridiculously pleased grin. She lavished in the dark sparkle of his eye, a rush of lust bursting through her every synapse. Splayed out below him, she writhed in tune with his shadowy appendages, trying to steal his control.

"You are mine," he whispered as though talking to himself.

"How many more ways can we bind ourselves together?"

"Careful, dear dreamer. You don't know what I'm willing to do." His dark words, undoubtedly true, were less threatening combined with the deep love in his eyes, which were alight with their orange glow.

"Then show me."

THE END

Thank you for reading! This story was close to my heart because of my own struggles with overcoming CPTSD and the multitude of sleep disturbances that come with. If you struggle with something similar, know that this author is rooting for you and believes it will get better.

Scan the QR code for all of my links! And keep flipping for a preview of Fallen for the Two-Headed Dragon.

Chapter 1
Dana

"You won't be fertile forever, you know. I really want us to start thinking seriously about our future family."

Jackson's words drifted past Dana through the mountain air, which was becoming more and more crisp as they made their ascent. This hiking trip through the Rockies was supposed to bring them closer together, but he kept spewing the same rhetoric about her *fertile eggs* as always and pushing her to get a job to support a nonexistent family.

"You should tell the temp agency tomorrow that you need something long-term and sustainable for kids, especially something with upward mobility. Ask about the maternity program."

"Okay."

"Are you even listening to me?" Jackson whirled on her. A rock scuttled from underneath his thickly treaded boot. Dana watched as it jumped over any pebbles in its way and passed between her feet to make a turbulent escape down the mountain pass.

"Of course I am, Jackson," she exasperated. She slipped her glasses off and wiped the lenses on her athletic tank top, causing even more streaks to line her eyesight when the plastic frames settled back onto her nose. She ignored them and walked past him with a practiced calm.

At this point in the three years they'd been together, she'd become an expert at tuning him out. Much like the way he tuned *her* out every time she reiterated that she didn't want kids. The cosmos only knew who was winning the argument, although it appeared Jackson had already decided.

She was as afraid of dying alone as the next person, but that wasn't the reason she stuck around. Jackson had supported her as she followed her passion for writing. At least financially, he'd supported her dreams of authorhood while she made very little income to contribute. If not for him, she would be living with her mom and sister in her hometown of Witmore, likely driving to and from Colorado Springs with a part-time job and writing only when she had the time.

She owed Jackson a great deal for how much he'd done for her. If not for her sense of guilt and duty, maybe she would have left. As it was, she was beginning to wear down.

They paused at the lowest peak on this trail, which was still a decent summit. Jackson slipped his arms around her waist from behind. The gesture was so gentle, she leaned into it and thought, *maybe I'm being ridiculous*. At twenty-seven years old, she knew plenty of women her age who were happy to be mothers. Her friend Cicily had an unexpected pregnancy and she constantly preached about it being the best thing to ever happen in her life.

Maybe it could be that way for Dana, too.

Jackson sighed. "This view is great. The only thing that would make it better would be if my hands were resting all the way out *here*"—he held his hands out as though her belly were bigger than a basketball—"instead of this flat strip."

"Right, like I would be climbing mountains if I were a whale," she snorted. Leave it to Jackson to remind her exactly why she didn't want to waver on the kids thing just as she was considering giving in.

Thankfully, Jackson was utterly predictable and couldn't go a full five minutes without reminding her she was a baby farm. With a shake of her head, she reached for her glasses as he retreated from her backside. It must be the altitude messing with her head, tricking her into believing his little gestures could be anything other than ploys to get his way.

The ground scraped under his feet somewhere behind her. His hands firmly met her shoulder blades and he grunted with effort as he shoved her off the mountain.

There was no time for anger or shock. Wind surged past with too much force for her limbs to fight, the noisy rush deafening. She hardly registered that she was falling, but her body took the beating of the cliffside. Not far down, she hit a slab of flat cliff with enough force to steal the breath from her lungs. The impact slowed her descent significantly and she slid, then tumbled on her side until she reached brush. She rolled and rolled, her whole body scraping and chafing as she bowled through the brush.

Her body was limp and battered by the time she reached level ground, rolled down a small incline, and plummeted deep into a bear cave.

"Asshole!" she shouted when she realized she was alive. Every bone and muscle in her body screamed with pain, her synapses on fire. The fact that she was alive was a miracle.

"That cock-sucking *bajingan*! *Jancok kon*!"

She lay still and checked in with her body. Her elbow felt funky and didn't want to move from its crooked position. That's fine, she could live without an arm, right? Blood covered her in many places, a whole chunk of skin missing from her thigh. It was grotesque to look at but didn't feel broken. It would definitely get uglier before healing.

If not for the cliff a couple yards down breaking her fall along with her tuck-and-roll skills, she would have died. Had that been Jackson's plan for this trip all along? Or had it been a spur of the moment thing? Agree to have his babies or die, apparently. She'd narrowly dodged that bullet. Moments before he pushed her, she'd truly considered giving in. That fucker almost got his way.

Her aching muscles revolted as she lugged herself into a seated position. With a full-body wince, she reached for her glasses but came up with empty air. *Great! Just what I need.* She would have to come up with money for new glasses on top of everything.

Okay, okay. She could do this. She just needed to climb out of the sloped tunnel and blindly find her way out of the woods. This was the same park they always hiked. She could get to the trail and find her way to the convenience store to call a car. Luckily, her pack and supplies seemed to have survived with her. If she made it home tonight, she could at least grab some personal items and her only remaining pair of contacts before heading to her mom's house in the morning. The bastard was probably going to continue his hike and stay at the lodge for the next couple nights as planned, because why not?

A large, strangely shaped red rock took up most of the discernible area of the cave, but there were piles of junk strewn about as well. Shiny objects glinted and vied for her unfocused eye. Peculiar items, sparkly things that wouldn't usually be found in an underground cave, even if someone were squatting there.

"Weird."

The textured rock moved. Two long, thick pillars of crimson extracted themselves from the main lump and moved forward, sending her scrambling back with a hiss of pain.

Two sets of eyes settled on her. Dana frantically looked between them, her neck whiplashing from side to side as all four eyes blinked slowly. A translucent membrane slid across the slitted irises followed by a heavy red lid. Both snouts dragged in deep breaths that commanded the air around her, sucking her tattered sleeves up toward them. Long, thin, forked pink tongues flicked out from both mouths, revealing double-lined rows of teeth as they dragged over dry lips.

Dana screamed. She catapulted out of there as fast as she could. She ignored the blazing hot pain in her elbow as she leaned on it to climb and the searing open wound of her leg as she stumbled.

She ran and ran and didn't look back, too terrified to consider that there were other things in these woods willing to eat her.

Chapter 2
Rathym

Fire was always a mesmerizing subject to Rathym. As a Fireborn, he'd grown up steeped in the traditions of the Great Flame. Fire poured from his throat with a familiar burn as he used the flames to rebuild and reshape the mountain. Fireborn were notoriously strong-willed and stubborn, forces to be reckoned with just like their element.

With the assistance of an ancient potion, Fireborn had been using their fire to hide in plain sight for millennia. Although the mountain rock was not hot to his touch, it glowed under his flames like embers of lava. Their bright orange mimicked the package aglow in the corner of his eye, mocking him with every glance he sent its way.

This latest mountain was more malleable than the ones before. The solid rock above him thundered and groaned under his ministrations, the enormous formation working double-time to resist his changes.

Rathym would not be moving his lair again. This was the last time. He hadn't been alive for over five centuries just to lie down and surrender his hard-earned things. This new home would be his, his alone, for his remaining time alive. If the human population continued to encroach, he would raze their cities to the ground. He would not consider returning to his traitorous homeland, not even if his stomach turned to ice and no fire graced his mouth again.

Besides, his collection of valuables had grown so massive that it was a pain to keep lugging around to new mountains.

Not that he didn't love sorting through his belongings. He did. He enjoyed the act of setting them up along the walls, creating shelving units in the stone to adorn with beautiful things, sorting the rest into piles. He loved to reminisce over his cherished treasures.

He *didn't* love to reminisce about his past. The shimmering orange summons hummed from its discarded spot on the dining table. The ghosts that haunted him had spent centuries looming in the back of his mind, but now they threatened to implode their thresholds.

With an aggravated harrumph, Rathym nudged the magic-laced parcel onto the floor and swiftly kicked it under the table. He would deal with it later. Right now, his new home required his full attention. A convenient distraction.

A distraction he'd been reliant on for nearly a week. He would have to open the parcel soon and assess the importance of its contents. The Fire Council would not contact him now, two centuries after his hostile departure, if the circumstances weren't dire. It was possible that he'd already procrastinated too long, rendering any aid he could provide useless.

Fortunately, there was no one alive in that realm that he still felt a responsibility to save.

The new cave was large enough to accommodate an additional pile. An exciting venture. What should he categorize into the new space? Perhaps by rank of beauty? A pile for enchanted items already existed, as did elven treasures gifted to Rathym before the fall of the great species. Other piles included gold, silver, and things that were just rather neat. He was sure to come up with something.

He backed into a corner to examine his handiwork. It was adequate, but would be more aesthetically pleasing once he finished decorating.

His tail bumped something under the table. In his recklessness, he'd positioned the summons in a horrible place. He quickly moved his tail, but the damage was done. The parcel now bore a gash in its packaging. It would be a matter of time before the whole parcel vanished, whether he'd read it or not.

"Cursed flame!" Rathym swore as he downshifted and snatched the folder. There was no way to know how quickly it would disappear. That depended on how classified the information was. Of course, if he were still in possession of his council-appointed signet ring, he would be able to force the enchanted parcel to remain even after its expiration.

Unfortunately, his ring was long gone. Anything inside the thick folder would dissipate after whatever length of time the council had deemed appropriate.

A stack of papers almost an inch thick goaded him. What could they possibly want from Rathym that required this much parchment? He eased the first piece from the front and began to read.

Sir Rathym Odrydimere, Grand Commander of the Fire Sworn Elite Forces, Regent to the Young Princess of Elvendale...

"*Former,*" he grumbled.

A muffled scream alerted him to a presence near his home's entrance. He immediately shifted back into his larger form, prepared to stand his ground when the intruder descended.

These cozy living quarters came equipped with a hidden entrance—a hole disguised as a burrow. He'd decided it had to be his immediately. All the better to keep prying human pests away. Although it had been a challenge to load his hoard through. He'd had to make a sort of back entrance that he promptly destroyed with an intentional rockfall the following day, which rearranged much of the mountain into staggered cliffs.

The petrified scream hurtled down the tunnel entrance and landed with a painful sounding thud.

A new precious item for my collection.

Rathym was an old-fashioned dragon and understood perfectly what it meant when something fell into his lair.

Very slowly, he placed the stack of parchment on the table. Careful not to scare the puny thing, he stood perfectly still and observed their reaction to this unsettling new arrangement.

This new piece of treasure was enchanting indeed. Their features rivaled those of any elf from Elvendale. Other than their phenomenal bone structure, however, they seemed ill-equipped for survival. They fumbled around like a blind mouse searching for scraps at a picnic, not to mention their delicious scent was sure to draw the ravenous beasts from their depths in the woods.

After he was content that he'd spent enough time observing his new jewel and had provided it with adequate time to adjust, he leaned in for closer inspection.

A human of female persuasion. He dragged in a deep breath of her scent to confirm. Yes, it was a distinctly powerful female pheromone. Even as a sweaty musk, it smelled so tantalizing he couldn't help but lick his lips.

She shrieked and clamored away, crawling awkwardly and inefficiently out of his entryway.

The little human ran from his lair, undoubtedly believing they'd made their escape.

Made in the USA
Monee, IL
26 April 2024